P9-DMW-012

"How is it that we went all these years without talking, Jude?"

"You have no idea how many times I've asked myself that same question," he said.

"Why didn't you...try?" she said.

"I could ask you the same thing."

The air stilled. Their words threatened to conjure the hurts of the past, and they tried to crowd between them.

"When the man who had asked you to give up everything and elope with him—to spend the rest of your life with him—shows up three months later engaged to someone else, it makes it a little hard to be the first one to reach out."

He nodded. "Fair enough. That's why I came to see you first thing when I got into town."

"This was probably a bad idea." She started to push to a sitting position, but with a strong arm, Jude pulled her down next to him.

"No, it's not."

And he kissed her.

* * *

CELEBRATION, TX:
Love is just a celebration away...

Dear Reader,

Part of my writing process includes making a playlist for each book I write. I listen to the songs when I'm not writing. They keep me "in the story."

The music I've chosen for *The Cowboy Who Got Away* makes one of my all-time favorite playlists. Particularly the song "The House That Built Me" by Miranda Lambert. It captures Jude Campbell's angst about coming home to Celebration, Texas, after being away for a decade and not achieving his goals the way he thought he would before he returned.

This cowboy got a taste of fame and fortune, but it was fleeting. After going home, he realizes that maybe a second chance at love with his high school sweetheart, Juliette Lowell, is worth more than the pot of gold at the end of the elusive rainbow. Maybe Juliette can help him believe he really can go home again—and stay.

If you'd like me to email you links to the playlist for this book, please email me at nrobardsthompson@yahoo.com or private message me on Facebook at Facebook.com/nrobardsthompson. Also, I hope you'll join me on Instagram at Instagram.com/nancyrthompson and Twitter at Twitter.com/NRTWrites. I'd love to hear from you!

Warmly,

Nancy

The Cowboy Who Got Away

Nancy Robards Thompson

HARLEQUIN® SPECIAL EDITION®

If you purchased this book without a cover you should be aware that this book is stolen property. It was reported as "unsold and destroyed" to the publisher, and neither the author nor the publisher has received any payment for this "stripped book."

Recycling programs
for this product may
not exist in your area.

ISBN-13: 978-0-373-62377-8

The Cowboy Who Got Away

Copyright © 2017 by Nancy Robards Thompson

All rights reserved. Except for use in any review, the reproduction or utilization of this work in whole or in part in any form by any electronic, mechanical or other means, now known or hereinafter invented, including xerography, photocopying and recording, or in any information storage or retrieval system, is forbidden without the written permission of the publisher, Harlequin Enterprises Limited, 225 Duncan Mill Road, Don Mills, Ontario M3B 3K9, Canada.

This is a work of fiction. Names, characters, places and incidents are either the product of the author's imagination or are used fictitiously, and any resemblance to actual persons, living or dead, business establishments, events or locales is entirely coincidental.

This edition published by arrangement with Harlequin Books S.A.

For questions and comments about the quality of this book, please contact us at CustomerService@Harlequin.com.

® and TM are trademarks of Harlequin Enterprises Limited or its corporate affiliates. Trademarks indicated with ® are registered in the United States Patent and Trademark Office, the Canadian Intellectual Property Office and in other countries.

Printed in U.S.A.

www.Harlequin.com

National bestselling author **Nancy Robards Thompson** holds a degree in journalism. She worked as a newspaper reporter until she realized reporting "just the facts" bored her silly. Now that she has much more content to report to her muse, Nancy loves writing women's fiction and romance full-time. Critics have deemed her work "funny, smart and observant." She resides in Florida with her husband and daughter. You can reach her at nancyrobardsthompson.com and Facebook.com/nancyrobardsthompsonbooks.

Books by Nancy Robards Thompson

Harlequin Special Edition

Celebration, TX

A Bride, a Barn, and a Baby
The Cowboy's Runaway Bride

Celebrations, Inc.

His Texas Christmas Bride
How to Marry a Doctor
A Celebration Christmas
Celebration's Baby
Celebration's Family
Celebration's Bride
Texas Christmas
Texas Magic
Texas Wedding

The Fortunes of Texas: The Secret Fortunes

Fortune's Surprise Engagement

The Fortunes of Texas: Welcome to Horseback Hollow

Falling for Fortune

The Fortunes of Texas: Whirlwind Romance

Fortune's Unexpected Groom

Visit the Author Profile page
at Harlequin.com for more titles.

This book is dedicated to my brother, Jay,
who has the best sense of humor of anyone I know.
Love you, little brother!

Special thanks to Ryder Bliss for helping me
name the antiques store in downtown Celebration.

Chapter One

"This is a *disaster*," the bride-to-be wailed. "I don't understand how you can be so calm when it's all your fault, Juliette."

Juliette Lowell bit the insides of her cheeks and resisted the urge to help Tabatha Jones, the bridezilla du jour, put her current crisis into perspective. Around the world, people less privileged faced life-and-death crises. The realization that the hand-dyed lavender pumps were two shades lighter than the bridesmaids' dresses was certainly a disappointment, but it was not a disaster of meltdown proportions as the bride was making it out to be.

"You have to fix this." Tabatha's voice rose three octaves, pushing a tear out onto her cheekbone. It left a trail in her foundation as it meandered down her sullen face. "This is absolutely unacceptable. The wedding is a month away and I need to know how you are going to make this right."

Standing in the middle of the Campbell Wedding Barn, the venue for the ceremony, Tabatha's breath was quick and shallow as she glared at Juliette.

She seemed dangerously close to hyperventilating.

"Take a deep breath, Tabatha," Juliette said. The minute the words left her lips, she knew they were a mistake.

"Don't tell me how to breathe," she said through gritted teeth. "Just fix this."

All Juliette could do was shrug. Probably a good choice since every word she uttered seemed to be digging her deeper into trouble.

When Tabatha had noticed the discrepancy in color, she'd called Juliette, who'd suggested they meet at the wedding venue to view the shoes and dresses in the same light in which they'd be worn during the ceremony.

"Tabatha, they really don't look bad," Juliette said, holding a silk pump next to a dress in a ray of sunshine streaming through one of the barn's generous skylights. "Besides, the dresses are long and people aren't going to be looking at your bridesmaids' feet. They will be looking at their beautiful faces. No one will notice that the color isn't exactly the same."

Tabatha growled. She actually growled. A guttural sound in the back of her throat that started low, then exploded in a noise that sounded like a bark. For a split second, Juliette feared she might lunge at her.

Tabatha's mother must have had the same worry because she put an arm around her daughter, but Tabatha brushed her off and pointed at Juliette. "The bridesmaids' shoes were custom-made in Italy."

"I know," Juliette said. "I told you that due to variations in dye lots and the different material of the shoes and dresses that the color might not be an exact match."

The woman had been so smitten by the thought of buying her bridesmaids bespoke shoes that she obviously hadn't heard a word that Juliette had said.

Or she had selective memory.

Juliette held up the shoe again, turning it every which way in the light. "It's close—"

"It's not close enough," Tabatha hissed. "All I care about is how you're going to fix this in time for the wedding. Fix it."

Tabatha thrust the lavender shoe at Juliette and walked out of the barn.

"Oh, Tabatha. Honey…" Her mother cast an apologetic glance at Juliette and trotted along after her daughter.

Good grief.

As Juliette stood there trying to digest what had just happened, another realization hit her hard. All her life she'd been a people pleaser. In the past, she would've chased after the client, falling all over herself trying to make the bride-to-be happy, promising her miracles she would've worked magic to deliver, but today, she just didn't have it in her.

She wanted Tabatha to have the wedding of her dreams, but the woman was out of control. She'd crossed the line. Juliette had told her about the possibility of color variations, but Tabatha had ignored her.

"I warned you," Juliette muttered under her breath as she slid the dress back into the garment bag and draped it over her arm. Before she placed the pumps back in their box, she held one up again and tried to look at the color with an objective eye. They were pretty. Well, as pretty as purple silk pumps could be.

Even so, her job was to make sure the bride was happy. She'd call her friend Nora at Sassy Feet Shoe Repair and see if she could help.

Juliette sighed. "It's a purple shoe. I don't know what more you want, Tabatha. The way you're acting, you'd think they sent you something chartreuse."

"Does Tabatha have something against chartreuse shoes?"

The familiar deep, masculine voice wound its way around her spine and settled at the very base of her solar plexus, making her breath catch and her heart do an all-too-familiar two-step. She knew it was Jude Campbell before she turned around and saw him standing in the wedding barn's doorway.

Her initial split-second reaction was *It's you. You're back.* She wanted to hug him and lose herself in the sanctuary of his strong arms, in the familiar feel and smell of him. But in the next blink, the intoxicating madness fell into the chasm that had been created by everything that had happened when they broke up and the ensuing years that they'd been apart since then.

"Actually, Tabatha dislikes *lavender* shoes. Or these lavender shoes, at least."

"Was that Tabatha I saw kicking up gravel as she peeled out of the parking lot?"

"Oh, she peeled out, did she? Nice. I hope she waited for her mother to get in the car and close the door before she sped off."

Jude nodded and flashed that effortless, brilliant smile that reached all the way to his brown eyes, making them crinkle at the corners. He looked exactly the same, from the top of his curly honey-brown hair to the broad, muscled shoulders all the way down to the toes of his weathered cowboy boots. Juliette's mouth went dry and all the reasons she should keep her walls firmly in place threatened to fly out the window, but she knew better.

She prided herself on only making new mistakes.

Jude Campbell, with his hypnotizing smile and those arms and broad shoulders, would not be a new mistake.

"Why are you here, Jude?"

He shifted his weight from one foot to another. "What's the matter, Juju? Aren't you glad to see me?"

"You're not allowed to call me that anymore."

Hearing him call her by the nickname he'd had for her all those years ago made something warm and forbidden blossom in her stomach.

Damn him. How was it that after all these years, after everything he'd done, he still had this effect on her? How could she still feel something for him after what he'd done to her? To *them*.

"You seemed like you were happy to see me when I was home for Ethan and Chelsea's wedding. What happened?"

Reality happened. Real life happened. Three months ago, he'd waltzed back into town for one night—for his brother's wedding to Juliette's best friend. He'd been the best man to her maid of honor. There had been a built-in safety in that short visit. Because of the wedding, almost every minute of her time had been consumed by helping Chelsea, or otherwise claimed by the schedule of events. There hadn't been enough time to let down her guard. But if she was honest with herself, in that short twenty-four hours the ice cap that had formed over her heart had started thawing.

He'd left so soon after the wedding there'd been no need to think about the feelings he'd stirred up in her. It wasn't denial; it was self-preservation. It had been ten years since he'd been back to Celebration. For all she knew, it would be another ten before he passed through again.

"You were *home*?" she said, emphasizing the operative word. "You breezed through so fast, I wasn't even sure if it was really you. Are you *home* longer this time, Jude?"

He cocked a brow. "Would you be happy if I said yes?"

Juliette didn't answer. She busied herself wrapping the purple shoe in the tissue paper it came in and putting it back into its box.

"I am home longer this time than last."

Damn if her gaze didn't find its way back to him. His eyes seemed to hold a mixture of bemusement and disappointment.

He wasn't that tall—just under six feet, which was

still big for a bull rider. But he had those broad shoulders and that lean, muscled body to compensate for it. He also had those lethal, dark brown eyes and that lopsided smile that had always disarmed her.

Even after everything that had happened, her former eighteen-year-old self whispered that she wouldn't mind a bit if he kissed her hello, but the twenty-eight-year-old she was now, the one who knew better, overruled that foolishness with a simple blink of her eyes.

This was the effect Jude Campbell had on every healthy, red-blooded woman he encountered.

And that's what she needed to remember.

"I'd heard through the grapevine that you weren't coming back for the ten-year reunion," she said.

"My plans have changed. Is it too late to change my RSVP?"

Juliette shrugged. "You'll have to call Marilyn Harding. She's chairing the reunion committee."

Juliette silently cursed Tabatha again. If not for the ridiculously demanding woman, she wouldn't have been at the Campbell Wedding Barn at the precise moment Jude had chosen to make his entrance. Juliette was a wedding planner, but Jude's sister, Lucy, owned and operated the venue. She had inherited the property after her parents had died several years ago and had turned the old ramshackle barn into one of the South's premier wedding barns.

Since Juliette sent so much business Lucy's way, she'd given Juliette a key to the place so that she could come and go as she needed. No sense in both of them being at the mercy of the gaggle of bridezillas who contracted Juliette to create the wedding of their dreams.

Lately, it seemed like every single bride she worked with turned into a bridezilla.

Juliette took a deep breath as she pondered the possibility that if every one of her brides seemed like a bridezilla, maybe they weren't the problem; maybe *she* was the one who'd gone off the rails. Or something like that. Maybe she was mixing her metaphors. She was so burned-out lately, it was a wonder she could even think. It didn't help that Jude was standing right there in front of her.

"I thought the homecoming queen would've been in the middle of organizing the ten-year reunion," he said.

Juliette frowned and hitched up the garment bag onto her arm. "So, you think the homecoming queen should plan the party, and the homecoming king should just be able to show up? And until today you weren't even sure if you could make it. Can you please explain the logic in that?"

Jude was silent for a moment and it took everything in Juliette's power not to fill the stillness, until finally, he spoke.

"Was there ever any logic when it came to you and me, Juju?"

Juliette's stomach clenched.

"If you are here to see Lucy, she's not in right now. You might want to give her a call on her cell phone. There's not an event tonight, so she and Zane were taking the day off."

"I've already talked to my sister. I stopped by because I saw your car out there."

She tried to ignore the satisfaction his confession brought her and almost asked him how he knew it was her car, but stopped short. He'd seen it when he was home for the wedding. Jude had taken a break from the professional bull riding circuit to come home for the wedding of his older brother, Ethan, to Chelsea Ashford Alden. Of course, that's when he'd seen it. The wedding had been the first time that she'd seen Jude in the nearly ten years since the two of them had broken up before she'd gone to college and he'd gone off to try out his skills on the PBR circuit.

He was fresh off a world championship win. A hometown hero. Of course he'd want to come home and bask in the glory.

"How long are you home?" she asked.

He shrugged. "Two or three weeks? A month? Depends."

All kinds of questions filled her head. It was the beginning of October. The PBR circuit usually ran through the end of the month. She wanted to ask him about work, but a sixth sense warned her that might be shaky territory. Really, it was none of her business. If he was still in the running for this year's championship, he wouldn't be hanging around Celebration right now. It stood to reason that she was better off not asking.

"Where are you staying?" she asked instead.

"At the cabin on the lower forty of my folks' property— my property," he corrected.

Jude and his siblings had inherited the ninety acres that had been in the Campbell family for three generations. They'd subdivided the property into three equitable shares. Ethan and Lucy each had working businesses on their respective properties.

"It's been a long time since you've been out there," Juliette said. "Are you comfortable there? Does the place even have electricity?"

"I have no idea. I'll be fine," he said. "If it's too bad, I can always crash at Lucy's."

"I wasn't offering you a place to stay," she said. She meant to be funny, but it came out sounding defensive.

"No? Too bad, because I just realized that Zane is probably crashing at my sister's. Ethan and Chelsea are newlyweds. You were my last hope to save me from being a third wheel."

He winked at her and she wasn't altogether convinced that he was kidding.

"Yeah, well, I have two words for you—Celebration Inn. I'm sure they have a vacancy. But wait. Have you not even been to the cabin yet? Otherwise you'd know if the electricity was turned on."

"Just rolled into town and saw your car."

He smiled at her, holding her gaze for a few beats too long as she realized that he'd stopped to see her first, before his family, before getting settled in.

"It's good to see you, Juju." He shifted from one foot to another. "If you're free, want to go grab a beer?"

Yes.

She shook her head. "It's eleven thirty, Jude. And

don't tell me it's five o'clock somewhere. If I drink now, I won't get anything done today."

He nodded. "Fair enough. How about a cup of coffee then?"

Whoever said *you can't go home again* didn't know what the hell they were talking about, Jude thought as he opened the door to the Redbird Diner for Juliette. The place hadn't changed a bit. Same red vinyl booths and light gray Formica tables. The bar that separated the grill from the dining room was done in the same red-and-gray color scheme it had always sported. Large framed posters of the food offerings—burgers, fried chicken, tuna melts, French fries, sodas and shakes, coffee and pie—lined the walls, and on top of each table, small jukeboxes waited for diners to choose their own music at the same bargain price they'd charged for as far back as he could remember—a nickel a song.

An old Johnny Cash standard filled the diner, which was uncharacteristically empty except for them and a busboy he didn't recognize cleaning a table.

The homey smell of the food made his stomach rumble. He realized it had been a while since he'd eaten. He'd been so eager to get back to Celebration, he hadn't bothered to stop and eat.

The sameness of it all warmed him in a way he hadn't expected. It must have been at least nine years since he'd been here. There'd been no time to stop in at the diner when he'd come back for Ethan and Chelsea's wedding.

The last time he'd been home before that had been for his mom's funeral.

His dad had died from injuries in a drunk driving accident ten months before his mom had passed. His dad had been the careless drunk. The wreck had left his mom in a wheelchair and she'd never fully recovered.

Jude had been there to bury his mother, but he hadn't bothered to come for his old man's funeral.

He had no idea why he was letting the old drunk haunt him now. They hadn't gotten along. During their last bad blowup, he'd punched Jude in the face and had sent him packing. Jude hadn't pressed charges because his mother had begged him not to. It was the first time the old man had ever turned violent. That was the only reason Jude hadn't taken it to the sheriff. But even though he hadn't involved the law, he had left town, not giving them a chance to talk it out or make amends.

Jude hadn't kidded himself. He'd deserved his father's anger. He just hadn't expected the black eye.

There was nothing he could do about it now. So, he blinked away the thought and put his hand on the small of Juliette's back as they walked to the booth in the back corner and seated themselves in the very same place they had spent many hours when they were in high school. Being here with her felt like stepping back in time. The diner was virtually unchanged and Juliette looked almost exactly the same as she had all those years ago—only better, if that was possible. His gaze swept over her face, taking her in. Her olive skin had the same healthy tanned glow. Her long dark silky hair hung loose around her shoulders, tempting him to reach out and touch it. And he could still get lost in those sky blue eyes that were intently watching him watch her. Yeah, definitely better. She was even more beautiful now than she used to be back then. It was a more seasoned beauty—a confidence that suggested she was comfortable in her own skin.

Time had definitely been good to her.

He smiled at the thought.

"What?" she asked, picking up the menu but not opening it.

He shook his head, dismissing her question.

"From my vantage point," she said, "that looked like a whole lot more than nothing."

This was definitely the same Juliette—the one who never let him get away with anything.

"I was just thinking," he said, "it's good to see you."

"It's good to see you, too." She sounded a little shy.

He rubbed his nail over a piece of worn duct tape that appeared to be covering a rip in the booth's red vinyl seat. The sensation grounded him, bringing him back to something that was hard and real and a little rough around the edges after standing the test of time. He identified with that. There was something both comforting and disquieting about finding himself in this diorama of the past.

How had they let so much time go by without speaking? The quick answer was that they were both stubborn. They'd both had their fragile teenage pride hurt. They'd gone off on different life paths and blinked and here they were again—all these years later. Jude was tempted to ask her to tell him everything—everything he'd missed, everything she'd grown to be. He had no idea if she was even dating anyone. For all he knew, she might be head over heels for someone else—she might not have even given him a second thought during the time that they'd been apart.

When they'd reconnected at Ethan and Chelsea's wedding, he'd stayed in Celebration less than twenty-four hours. It was all he could spare from the circuit—but even with the limited interaction, it was enough time to realize that he and Juliette still had chemistry. Even after all these years.

That revelation was one of the driving forces behind his decision to come home after the concussion and back injury that had knocked him out of the running for the professional bull riding finals. He was doing better, but sometimes he woke up with blinding headaches and his body hurt like he was one hundred years old. Still, he wasn't going to tell her that. He was too young to complain about his aches and pains that no one wanted to hear about, anyway.

"So, tell me everything," Juliette said. Those blue eyes of hers sparkled and made his mind go temporarily blank.

"Everything?" he asked. "That's a tall order."

"Everything. Just start from the beginning."

The beginning? As in when he'd proposed and she'd turned him down? Or did she want him to skip ahead to the part where he'd gotten engaged to somebody else and Juliette had vowed to never speak to him again. She'd done a pretty good job of keeping that promise, until he'd seen her at the wedding.

And now here they were. At least they were talking. He toyed with the corner of the plastic laminated menu. "Everything is a lot of ground to cover. We could be here for a while."

He hadn't realized what a loaded statement that was until he saw her brow arch ever so slightly and the faint smile that turned up the outer corners of that gorgeous mouth. What he would give to know what was going on in her mind at that moment.

He mustered his best smile. "Judging by the look on your face, you don't have plans this afternoon?"

"That remains to be seen," Juliette quipped. "Start talking and we'll see."

Her sassy mouth was one of the things he'd loved best about her. Well, that and about a million other things that were coming back to him one by one.

Funny, over the past ten years he'd attracted a certain type of woman who had been happy to let him call the shots and set the pace. Juliette had always held her own with him and he'd forgotten how damn attractive that was. He was just about to ask her if she was seeing anyone when she spoke first.

"How about starting with why you're home, and at the beginning of October. The season isn't over. Shouldn't you be off at some competition showing a bull who is boss?"

Oh, that.

"One of the reasons I'm home is because someone's interested in buying my land," he said. "I've had an offer on it."

She leaned forward. "You're thinking about selling your part of the Campbell ranch?"

He nodded, but before he could say anything else, Dottie Wilde, who had worked at the Redbird Diner for as far back as Jude could remember, walked up with her order pad and a broad smile plastered across her face.

"Well, if it isn't Jude Campbell, as I live and breathe. Honey, is that really you?"

He flashed his best smile and winked. "Yes, ma'am, Mrs. Wilde. It's me."

She leaned in and gave him a hug.

"When did you get home, honey?"

"About an hour ago."

She put her hand on her heart. "Oh, my stars, I am honored to be your first stop back in the old neighborhood."

His gaze snagged Juliette's. "If I'm completely honest, the Redbird is my second stop."

Mrs. Wilde turned her smile on Juliette. "Well, silly me. Of course you'd go see your girl first. It just warms my heart to see you kids together again. Just like old times. Makes me feel young again."

He looked at Juliette, who wasn't looking at him. She had politely smiled at Dottie and then had taken a keen interest in the menu, reminding him that even though they were talking and she had agreed to have coffee with him, even though that undeniable chemistry still pulsed between them, a chasm the size of the Grand Canyon still separated them.

He looked back at Dottie, who was making a show

of brushing away happy tears, but she shook off her reverie and beamed at them.

"Look at me," she said. "Aren't I a sight? I'm a bundle of emotions today. What'll you have? It's all on the house. Anything you want. It's not every day we have a professional bull riding celebrity wander in here. You're our very own hometown hero and that calls for a celebration."

They ordered coffee and a piece of blueberry pie to share. The Redbird Diner had always had good pie.

After Dottie left to round up the food, Juliette said, "Well, Cowboy, aren't you something. I guess it pays to be a *hometown hero*. In all the years I've been coming here, I've never gotten free food from Dottie Wilde."

He shrugged. "Her offer is nice. But totally unexpected. I'll leave her a big tip."

All this hometown hero talk made him uncomfortable.

He'd won the PBR world championship last year. But this current season, he'd done nothing but struggle and battle one injury after another. Last year, before he'd won the big prize, all his hard work had paid off and his plans had come to fruition. Everything had snapped into place. Since then, it seemed as if every force was working against him. At twenty-eight, he was one of the senior members of the circuit. He'd worked damn hard to get there, but this year, it seemed like his reflexes weren't as quick to respond; sometimes his instincts seemed to lag behind. Talk had been that his head just wasn't in the game. The truth was his body just didn't seem to bounce back the way it had leading up to his win.

Because of all the setbacks, he was out of the running for the big money this season. He'd come back to Celebration to sort it all out. To figure out if he was up for one more good run or if he should quit before he suffered permanent damage like the doctors had warned.

His agent insisted that the doctors had to be overly cautious to avoid liability. He kept reminding Jude that a lot of guys got right back on the bulls after getting hurt. When Jude had hesitated, he reminded him that because of his age and injuries the clock on his career was ticking and he needed to make hay while the sun was shining. The subtext to that, of course, was that the sun hadn't been smiling down on him much this year.

The chime on the door sounded and three girls who looked like they were high school age entered the diner and settled in the booth next to the one he and Juliette occupied. One of them was in Jude's line of sight and she smiled at him. He smiled back, just being polite.

"You're not really going to sell your property, are you?" Juliette asked, a frown knitting her brows.

When their parents had died, he, Ethan and their sister, Lucy, had each inherited equally valued parcels of land. Ethan's was smaller, but had the stables from which he ran his horse-breeding business. Several decades ago, his family's ranch had been one of the most successful in the area, but they'd run into financial hardship when alcoholism had gotten the best of Donovan Campbell. For a while it appeared that Ethan might fall down the same slippery slope after his parents' deaths and the end of his first marriage, but after some soul searching and sheer determination, he'd pulled himself up from rock bottom and had set the Triple C Ranch back on the road to profitability.

Lucy had the parcel where their grandparents' old house and barn stood. She'd spent a lot of time there as a child, so it seemed only right that that portion of the property would be hers. She'd moved into the house and had worked hard to turn her dream into a reality when she'd transformed the old abandoned barn into the Campbell Wedding Barn, one of the South's premier boutique venues.

The land Jude had inherited was on the outer edge of the property. It was mostly wide-open pasture, but it did contain two structures, an old cabin near a lake and a bungalow, that the late mother of Lucy's fiancé, Zane Phillips, had rented for decades before her passing. The rent Dorothy Phillips had paid had helped cut the cost of maintaining the property and lifted the burden of property taxes. Now the place was sitting vacant, and without the rental income, Jude was concerned about the place becoming a financial drain—especially since this year's earnings paled in comparison to last year's.

Sure, he was all about family legacy—in theory—but the bottom line of his budget and slowly shrinking bank account made the opportunity to unload the property seem attractive.

"I don't know if I'm going to sell," he said. "That's what I came home to figure out."

"Excuse me?" The girl who had smiled at him a

moment ago was standing next to their table. "Are you Jude Campbell?"

He sent a look to Juliette that he hoped said, *Sorry about this.*

"That would be me," he said.

"I'm a huge fan. In fact, I bought this shirt because it's a Copenhagen On-Off Shirt."

Copenhagen was the sportswear manufacturer who sponsored him. The On-Off Shirt had materialized after a particularly rough ride his championship year. After going ten seconds on a mean bull, the beast not only bucked him off, but charged after him. Jude narrowly sidestepped the animal, but not before one of the bull's horns caught the edge of his shirt, ripping it off and leaving him to run for his life bare-chested.

The best ride of Jude's life had been overshadowed by a bull stripping off his shirt. A video clip had gone viral and the graphic of him, naked from the waist up, had turned into a sensation that inspired his own line of shirts, the On-Off Shirt.

As far as he was concerned, they were just plain old shirts. They weren't breakaway style, they didn't go on and off any easier than a regular run-of-the-mill T-shirt, but fans—old and new—had scooped them up like they were gold. At least for a little while. As of late, thanks to a combination of the public's fickle attention span and his lackluster performance this season, sales were on the downturn. His agent, Bob Bornfield, was desperately trying to renegotiate the terms of the endorsement contract.

One element on which Jude wouldn't budge was the

part that obligated Copenhagen to donate 10 percent of net sales to a charity that benefited at-risk teens.

Then again, 10 percent of nothing equaled nothing.

"Would you sign it for me? My name is Shari." She brandished a black permanent marker. Her blond hair was slicked back into a tight, high ponytail, and she wore hoop earrings the size of doughnuts and a ton of makeup. It looked like she'd used the marker to line her eyes.

"Sure," Jude said.

"Right here." Shari touched the top of her left breast and leaned in, giving Jude all access. "S-H-A-R-I," she spelled as she tapped her breast.

Jude blanched. This girl was much too young to be suggesting what it seemed like she was. He glanced at Juliette, who was busy fishing coins out of a small purse she'd pulled from her handbag.

This was awkward.

Jude would be lying if he didn't admit that things like this happened frequently when he was on the road. Except usually the women were, well, *women*. Not teenage girls.

In the context of a rodeo, it seemed like part of the job—part of the show. He'd flirt, they'd flirt back, he'd sign autographs—yes, sometimes bare midriffs and cleavage—and make small talk with various degrees of innuendo. It was all in fun and part of the free-spirited cowboy image he'd cultivated: Jude Campbell, the face—and bare chest—of the Copenhagen On-Off Shirt. Most of the time the women would move along. And sure he had the occasional groupie hang around until everyone had gone. Occasionally things happened. But he was single. Completely unencumbered. The road could be a lonely place. But he always practiced safe sex. Always.

Sitting here with Juliette while this girl thrust her breast in his face was just…straight-up wrong. It felt disrespectful and sleazy.

He leaned back, away from the girl. Then he pointed to the cuff of the long-sleeved T-shirt. "I'll sign it here."

"No, really, here is better." She tapped her breast again.

"No, really. This is better." He tapped the sleeve with the marker.

Looking a little disappointed, she took a step back and offered him the inside cuff.

He signed and said in his most professional voice, "Thanks for your support, Shari."

Thank God the girl simply turned and went back to her table. After she was gone, Jude said, "Sorry about that."

"Hazard of the job, huh?"

"Something like that." His voice was an apology.

While he was signing the shirt, Juliette had dumped some coins on the table, separating three nickels from the rest of the money. Jude reached into his pocket and pulled out the little bit of change he had. It wasn't much, but he added five more nickels to the pile. Juliette fed them into the machine and punched in some numbers. The first tune that played was Luke Bryan's "To The Moon And Back." He had the CD in his truck.

"If you're serious about selling, couldn't you have

negotiated the sale through lawyers?" she asked after she'd finished choosing the music.

He blinked at the change of subject, but was relieved that she seemed unfazed by Shari—or at least was willing to move on.

"Yes, but I need to see the property again. My real estate agent said the buyer had some questions. Plus, I need to talk to Ethan face-to-face."

She nodded. "Probably a good idea. Something tells me he might not take this very well."

Juliette got it. She still understood his family dynamics. Sometimes she'd gotten it better than he had.

He was just opening his mouth to say as much when the door chime sounded again and his old high school buddy Tony Darcy walked in with two little kids in tow.

"Hey, Tony," Jude called. "What's going on, man?"

"Campbell? What the— What are you doing here?"

The two shook hands and exchanged quick man hugs. Tony greeted Juliette.

They made small talk, doing the cursory catch-up. Tony said he'd been following Jude's journey on the PBR circuit.

"I'm living vicariously through you, bro," he said.

Tony said he was teaching math at Celebration High School. He'd married his high school sweetheart, Janet Hayes, five years ago. They had two kids and Janet was ready to give birth to their third any day now.

"I'm glad I got to see you because with the baby on the way, Janet and I probably won't make it to the reunion. That's why you're back in town, right? How long are you in town?"

Jude shrugged. "That's up in the air right now. It just depends on some things that I have brewing."

"If you do end up staying for a while, would you be willing to come and talk to the high school's rodeo club? I'm the sponsor and I know they'd all love to hear from a champion. You're kind of a big deal around here. But don't get a big head or anything."

"Sure, I'd love to come and talk to them. Let me see what I have going and I'll give you a call."

They exchanged numbers, and by that time Dottie delivered the blueberry pie and coffee and Tony's to-go order, which he'd phoned in earlier. Tony paid and was out the door, but not before promising that if he didn't hear from Jude he'd come looking for him.

"Remember that bonfire party we had out by the lake on your property?" Juliette said, her eyes sparkling with humor. "Oh, my gosh, remember when Tony and Isaac Oppenheimer were being jackasses and decided to go skinny-dipping to embarrass all the girls?"

Jude laughed. "And someone went to hide their clothes and ended up dropping them in the fire by mistake."

Juliette was laughing so hard she had tears in her eyes. "And we had to make sandwich boards out of the beer boxes and bungee cords so that they didn't get arrested for indecent exposure. It would've served them right if they'd spent the night in jail. That makes me sound old, doesn't it?" She shook her head. "We had some good times out there, didn't we?" A faraway smile softened her features as she picked up her coffee cup.

Jude swallowed a bite of pie. "Remember that time

my dad was drunk when he was keeping watch out by the barn looking for those coyotes that kept trying to get after the horses? He almost shot me thinking I was an animal when really I was just sneaking in late for curfew."

"You were an animal." She laughed again and the sound washed over him like balm. "That's when I started calling you Wylie," she said. "Oh, and remember that tree we planted by the cabin? I wonder if it's still there."

"I don't know. Why don't you come out there with me and we'll find out?"

Chapter Two

Juliette should've said no when Jude asked her to come with him to the lake cabin. Reminiscing over coffee was one thing, but returning to the scene where they'd made most of their memories was entirely another.

Yet here she sat in his truck, right next to him in the very place that had been *her spot*. Of course, it was a different truck. It was newer and more expensive than the old beater Ford he'd driven in high school, but if she closed her eyes, she could see the two of them just as they were.

That's why she needed to keep her eyes wide-open and her head firmly in the here and now.

She knew better than this. If she was tempted to forget why letting down her defenses with Jude was a bad idea, all she had to do was remind herself what happened with Shari at the Redbird Diner. Witnessing that girl fawning all over him had conjured the same feelings someone throwing a bucket of ice water in her face would have. It had been enough to shock some sense into her. Of course, it wasn't Jude's fault that women found him irresistible. She had to give him credit for handling Shari as well as he did. The girl seemed to offer herself to him the same way that Dottie had offered free pie—it was his for the taking. That was the life of an unmarried bull riding champion. Jude and his groupies were a package deal. She needed to keep that in mind when she found herself getting swept up in the current of his charisma.

She stole a glance at his profile as he steered his truck off the gravel drive and down the dirt path that led to the lake. The problem was, all she had to do was spend a little time with him and all of yesteryear's feelings threatened to flood back, making her feel like she was a teenager again and so in love that she couldn't tell her own wants from his. She couldn't distinguish the boundaries between his life and hers.

Because back then, there had been no boundaries.

She wasn't in love with him anymore, but that chemistry, that electricity that had been the hallmark of their relationship, was still there, stronger than ever. She was pretty sure if she reached out and touched him that the air would sizzle.

And that's why she needed to watch herself.

The truck bumped along the grooves that had worn into the carpet of green grass. They passed groups of skinny pine trees and the occasional cluster of rocks and boulders. Finally, Jude stopped between the big live oak where the two of them had carved their initials on one of those endless summer nights and the old cabin that had served as their lakeside cabana.

They used to sneak off down here and disappear into their own little world. Everything else would fade away, except for them. God, they'd been two crazy teenagers who had been so hot for each other they couldn't keep their hands to themselves. But even before that—when they were younger and more innocent—they'd always been drawn to each other. They'd rode horses together on his family's ranch. He'd taught her how to barrel race and she'd taught him the difference between a salad fork and a dinner fork. He'd held her and let her cry on his shoulder when her dad died. She'd given him advice about how to make his relationship with his own dad better. She was his girl. He was her guy. She couldn't even remember when exactly they'd made their relationship official. They just always *were*.

Jude and Juliette.

Juliette and Jude.

Juju.

Juju was interchangeable for them collectively or for each of them separately—one of the sickeningly sweet pet names they'd had for each other.

It had all been great. Until it wasn't anymore and ten years of silence had stretched between them like an endless ocean cloaked by night.

"The place looks good," Jude said, leaning forward to look out the windshield and glance around. "Ethan has been looking after it for me."

Juliette took off her seat belt and shifted so that she was facing him. It would've felt so natural to slide over next to him and tuck herself into that nook under his arm where she'd always fit so perfectly.

But no. That was the danger zone.

"Did you not make arrangements to have someone else take care of the place?"

Jude nodded. "Of course I did. I paid the upkeep bills. He just offered to help. You know Ethan."

She hadn't meant to sound judgmental. Even though she felt proprietary, the place wasn't hers and whatever arrangement Jude and Ethan had agreed to wasn't her business. As an only child, she didn't know the luxury of leaning on a sibling. She certainly hadn't been out here to look after the place. Not since…that night.

That fateful night. It had all unfolded in the cabin. She hadn't realized when she'd come out here searching for Jude that her whole world would change. Or maybe she had. Maybe having a big blowup was the only way she could've left.

No, she wasn't going there. The best way to get herself back on track was to make a joke. "I mean, think of all the hooligans who might come out here and party and skinny-dip and get into all kinds of trouble."

Jude nodded. "Exactly. I'm sure they'll thank me later."

Playing along, Juliette rolled her eyes. "I'm sure they will."

They got out of the truck and started walking down toward the lake.

"Oh, my gosh," Juliette said, pointing to a tall tree near the lake bank. "Is that the sapling?"

"It has to be," Jude said. It was the only tree between the lake and the cabin that wasn't ancient. "Looks like it not only survived, but it's thriving."

"I'm so glad it's still here," she said. "We planted that, Jude. You and me. Look at it. It's beautiful."

He was looking at her like she was an angel. "At least we did something right. I think it's a sign."

She narrowed her eyes. "A sign of what?"

He smiled a knowing smile. "A sign of good things to come."

She wanted to make a joke and ask him if he meant a sign of *good times* to come. But she couldn't bring herself to do it. A comment like that felt like she was offering more than she could deliver. There was a lot to sort out.

She was rarely at a loss for words, but as she stood there trying to figure out what to say, he turned and started heading toward the lake.

The warm breeze played with her hair and danced on the water, creating gentle ripples. It was the perfect day to be outside. Closer to the spot where the grass gave way to a dirt embankment, the rustling leaves of the river birch whispered a sweet welcome-home greeting. The grass looked as if it had been freshly mowed and the water weeds were so neat, they must've been trimmed recently.

A few feet in front of them, a black snake slithered by.

Juliette let out a little yelp as she jumped back and

grabbed onto Jude's arm. The move was a reflex and she pulled away as soon as she realized how good he smelled.

"Snake." She grimaced. "You know how I feel about snakes."

He smiled. "I remember. But don't worry, that black snake is harmless. Even though there are other creatures around here who aren't. Did we really used to take off all our clothes and swim in that water? At night—?"

"Were we stupid or what?" she agreed.

And crazy for each other.

They'd done a lot more than swim in that lake, but she wasn't going to remind him. She probably didn't need to.

The look that settled on his face told her that he was right there with her.

As if reading each other's minds, they smiled knowing smiles at each other. He was a gentleman and he didn't bring it up. She knew she should be grateful, but the teenager in her was disappointed.

"I need to check on a couple of things while I'm out here," he said. "This is one of them. The buyer's Realtor said the water level of the lake was way down and it was close to drying up. Looks fine to me. He also said there's a problem with that old foundation slab that my dad poured. Remember how he wanted to build an outbuilding to house the mowers and equipment? The buyer's agent is using the lake and the slab as reasons to undercut the offer."

As they walked toward the place where Don Campbell had poured the foundation for the project he hadn't been able to complete, Juliette said, "It sounds like they're playing hardball, Jude."

He shrugged. "You know, that's just how it goes in business."

"What kind of a business is the buyer in? Is it another rancher? Did Zane tell you that he sold his ranch to Bridgemont Farms? They'd been after him for a while to sell and when Dorothy got sick he needed the money to help her out with her medical bills."

Zane Phillips was engaged to Jude's little sister, Lucy. The pair was expecting a baby in a few months. If Juliette was a true romantic, Lucy and Zane's story might have made her believe that there was still hope for her and Jude. Lucy and Zane had been lifelong friends and had finally taken that friendship to the next level. Now they were expecting a baby.

But they had done things the right way. They had been friends *before* they became lovers. They knew each other inside and out and understood each other. Sure, she and Jude had history, but they also had a whole lot of standing water underneath their own bridge of years. Too much water, Juliette feared, to be able to bail themselves out and get to the other side without drowning if they decided to shed the superficial and dive into everything that had gone wrong.

When they got to the concrete slab, Jude stepped up onto it and then offered his hand to Juliette, helping her up onto the foundation. The block was weathered and cracked as expected for something that had been exposed to the elements for nearly a decade.

"It's not ideal, but it's not going to cost them twenty thousand dollars to remove it," Jude said.

"Twenty thousand dollars? Are you kidding me?"

"Like I said, they're playing hardball. They're saying that because the lake dried up it shouldn't be considered lakefront property. Since I don't live in Celebration anymore, I guess they thought I wouldn't check, which is pretty ridiculous."

"The lake is perfectly fine. Who are these con men?"

"I'm not altogether sure. My Realtor is dealing with them through their Realtor. She's the one handling the specifics. It's some corporation I've never heard of. I haven't had a chance to check them out because I've been so busy. I just haven't gotten to that point yet. And I wanted to check out their claims before I invested too much energy. But now that I'm back, once I get settled in and I can take a breath, I'll do my research."

Juliette nodded. At least he wasn't 100 percent set on selling to this buyer. She knew it was crazy, but the thought of him letting go of the property made her sad. It would feel as if he was divesting himself of the last bit of *them*. And that was selfish. Because if he had no use for the property, he still had to pay property taxes and such. Even so, the thought of it made her heart feel heavy. This was their place.

"Let me pull up the email from my Realtor." Jude took out his phone. "I think she mentioned who they are."

He tapped and scrolled the screen, then handed Juliette his cell.

"Here it is."

She took the phone, ignoring the way their hands brushed.

The email said:

Hi, gorgeous, the offer for the Celebration, Texas, property is attached. Call me if you have any questions. Or call me, even if you don't have any questions. Just call me. Smooches, Afton

"Smooches?" Juliette said before she could stop herself. "What kind of real estate professional signs her email 'smooches'?"

Jude laughed. "That's just Afton."

"Oh, well, Afton sounds like she likes you. Isn't there some sort of professional code of ethics she's violating? Like how doctors aren't supposed to get personally involved with their patients?"

"Afton and I are not personally involved."

"Really? Sounds like she thinks you are, *gorgeous*."

He laughed. It was a full-bodied belly laugh. "You're jealous." Even though the familiar sound of his laughter soothed her, she still felt heat blooming on her cheeks.

"I am not jealous." She raised her chin. "Why would I be jealous?"

"Because you still love me." He was teasing. She knew he was, the same way he used to always tease her. Since every word that came out of her mouth seemed to make it worse, she didn't answer him. Instead, she turned her attention to his phone. "Do you mind if I pull up the attachment that *Smooches* sent?"

"No, go ahead."

"So, wait, is she representing you or the buyer? Because it doesn't seem like *Smooches* has your best interests at heart."

"Why do you say that?"

"Because she should advise you not to let them undercut you with bogus claims."

He was smiling at her like she was adorable. And then he laughed. "I'm aware of their *bogus claims*. Afton is an old friend. She knows, too. She also understands that I'm on the fence about selling the property. I wasn't actively looking for a buyer. But she brought me the offer."

"But she knows you well enough to know you own the property. Is she an old girlfriend?"

"You *are* jealous."

Juliette handed him his phone. "Never mind. Forget I asked."

"You didn't look at the attachment."

Juliette shook her head. "I'll let you do the honors of opening it. Especially since you haven't looked at it yet. That has nothing to do with jealousy and everything to do with self-preservation. Who knows what other surprises *Smooches* might have in store for you."

His gaze flickered to hers. For a split second he looked like he wanted to say something, but he didn't. He honed in on his phone. "The offer is from an outfit called the MAG Holdings Limited Partnership. Never heard of them. Have you?"

Juliette shook her head. "Do an internet search and see what you can find out."

"It says here that MAG Holdings is the parent company for Metro Arrow Homes."

That didn't sound very good. "Jude, they build houses. Like those cookie-cutter shoeboxes that all look alike. If they want to put a subdivision in here, they can't. It's not zoned for single-family housing.

"They must have something up their sleeve," Juliette said. "Because I doubt that they'd be willing to fork over a lot of money to turn the property into a nature preserve. It's a nice idea, but I don't think so."

His brows knit together as he read the information that was on the screen. "This isn't okay. In fact, it's not going to happen."

He shook his head as he continued to read. "No, this is no good at all. Besides, with the way they're trying to undercut the asking price...I think this deal is off."

Both of them were silent, watching a couple of sandhill cranes fly in and land in the lake's shallow water near the shore.

"I think that's smart," Juliette said. "Judging by what they're trying to pull with the lake and the slab, it sounds like they aren't very honest."

"Yeah, there are few things I hate more than wheeler dealers," Jude said.

"Of course," Juliette said.

They walked in silence back the way they came. Juliette focused on the unchanged beauty of the place and tried not to wonder whether or not he'd ask Afton to look for another buyer. The lush green grass, the smattering of trees, the big live oak on the other side of the cabin, where they used to seek shade on hot summer days. It was like reuniting with an old friend or time traveling. If she squinted her eyes and blocked out everything else—especially the voices in her head—she was transported back to a much simpler time, when she and Jude were in love and their only worry had been not attracting the sheriff when they lit a bonfire on a cold fall night.

"Are you seeing anyone?" he asked out of the blue, breaking the silence.

The non sequitur made her breath catch. Really, the question shouldn't have been so surprising. It was an obvious question that old friends would ask each other. Although, they might start with the less important and build up to this. But, hey, leave it to Jude to take the leap.

"Who wants to know?" She raised her brows at him, trying to lighten the mood.

"I want to know, Jules."

"In this moment, I'm seeing you," she said, "walking next to me. That's all that matters."

He nodded. "Then I'll take that as a no, that you're not otherwise involved with anyone."

She put her hands on her hips. "What about you? Do you have someone special or is it just the Saturday night special…an endless line of Aftons?"

Okay, that was corny. She was trying to be funny, but obviously funny wasn't her thing.

"No, there's no one special in my life right now. And for the record, I don't have time for *Saturday night specials*, as you put it. What does that even mean?"

Juliette shrugged. "Random women. You know, a different Afton every Saturday night."

"Most Saturday nights I'm at a competition and by the time I'm done—after I've been tossed around, thrown and sometimes kicked or stepped on—this body is not always in the mood for a *Saturday night special*."

Juliette smiled. "That's good to know. I mean, it's not good that you get thrown and stepped on." She grimaced. "You know that's why I always had a hard time watching you compete. I couldn't stand to see you get hurt. You know, come to think of it, you never answered my question. What are you doing back in Celebration when there's still a month left on the tour? I know you said you were home to check out the property, but that doesn't take two weeks. In two weeks it will be time for the world championship. What's going on, Jude?"

He stiffened and crossed his arms over his chest. Defensive body language. But Juliette was determined not to speak first, because if she did it might give him an out—he might latch onto it and change the subject.

His gaze met hers. She raised her brows.

"I ran into some trouble. I got thrown a little too hard in a couple of matches and I had to sit out the next ones."

"Oh, no. Are you okay?"

Jude tore his gaze away from hers. He kicked at the dirt with the toe of his boot, as if giving himself more time to form his words.

"I suffered a couple of concussions. I couldn't ride because of it. Now I don't have enough points to qualify for the world championship." He cursed under his breath. "How about that? I'm the reigning world champion and I won't even be able to defend my title."

He laughed, but it was a dry and brittle sound.

She resisted the urge to hug him. "Jude, I'm proud of you for doing the right thing. Your health—your well-being—is so much more important than a competition."

His face fell. "It's my livelihood, Jules. It's not just a competition. It's what I do. It's what I'm good at. It's who I am."

"I get it, Jude. But if the doctor is telling you it's not a good idea for you to take the risk and ride, if you go against doctor's orders to do it, the repercussions could be..."

She shuddered. She couldn't bring herself to say the word—*deadly*. Even the thought of it made her heart hurt.

Jude shrugged. The look on his face said he didn't agree. They'd had this conversation about the risk of him getting hurt so many times when they were in high school—or at least variations of it.

Having been away from him all these years, she hadn't allowed herself to think about the reality of what he was doing every day, how he earned his living. The risk he faced every day. Sure, she'd kept up with him. She'd been happy to read about the results of his competitions. The internet was a beautiful thing in that regard. She loved seeing that he was doing well, seeing his steady climb to the top of his game. But reading the CliffsNotes also meant that she didn't have to see him get thrown and come within centimeters of getting stomped.

They'd always been at odds over this—for as far back as she could remember. And nothing had changed. It was best to change the subject.

Their gazes found each other and locked in a silent truce.

She could agree with that. She didn't want to fight with him. Not on the first day seeing him after all these years. She wasn't sure what his plans were. She had no idea if she was even going to get to see him very much while he was home. She realized in that moment that she wanted to. But still, they had this moment. Maybe that was all that mattered.

When they got back to the truck, Jude walked to the tailgate, opened it and started peeling back the bed cover.

"What are you doing?" she asked.

"I need to get my things out of here," he called over his shoulder.

"What things?"

"My suitcase. All the things I brought with me."

"So, you really haven't been here yet?"

"Nope. Just arriving."

That meant his first stop really had been to see her at the wedding barn. When he'd told Dottie that, she thought he would have at least stopped by the cabin and unpacked first.

As he unloaded, Juliette walked over to the ancient tree near the cabin, the one they'd carved their initials into.

"Remember this?" she said, tracing a finger over the

words etched into the rough bark, time-weathered and darkened like a wound that had left a scar.

Jude walked up behind her. "'Jude and Juliette 4-ever.'" His voice sounded hoarse and throaty. "And here we are again."

He set down his bags, reached out and traced the words the same way she had. Then he covered her hand with his. She stood there for a moment memorizing the warmth of his hand on hers.

"Jude."

He leaned in so close she could feel the heat of him, but she didn't turn around. She didn't pull away, either.

Instinctively, she knew if she turned around his lips would be much too close to hers. She might kiss him. She wanted to kiss him, wanted to taste his lips again and see if, like everything else out here, the taste of them, the feel of them, was still the same.

"I wanted to check on the sapling we planted, but I had forgotten about this tree," he said. "How could I forget it?"

She shrugged. The gesture seemed to pull him in closer. She could smell that Jude smell—a mixture of leather and citrus and grassy undertones. Usually, people were a product of their environment. How was it that so much time had gone by and Jude still smelled exactly the same? She breathed in deeply, turning her head toward him slightly.

The nearness of him made her shiver and relax into him. "It's still here. It stood the test of time," she whispered.

A long moment passed with his words hanging between them. "I'm glad you didn't forget about me, Jules."

If she didn't reclaim her personal space, she was going to do something she might regret.

Might regret.

Then again, she might not.

"You're pretty hard to forget."

It was eerie to find themselves back at the spot where everything had started. And ended. It was as if they were here for a do-over—or a second chance to make things right.

More than once, when she'd kissed another man, her mind had conjured Jude. Then the letdown she'd suffer when she opened her eyes to find herself in the arms of a familiar stranger would be devastating. The memory of Jude's kiss took her back. It was as if she was seeing everything that was once so familiar through brand-new eyes.

He turned her around. His arms slid around her. He pulled her close and placed a soft kiss on her lips. She put her hands on the sides of his face and anchored his mouth to hers. The kiss started slow and soft. But that lasted for a mere second before his arms tightened around her and he took possession of her mouth. Passion ignited a ravenous hunger. She parted her lips to deepen the kiss. She leaned into him as if her next breath depended on him.

For a moment, common sense upended and the whole world disappeared. He pulled her tighter, staking his claim, unspoken feelings pouring out in this wordless confession.

He tasted like blueberries from the pie they'd shared earlier and coffee and the cinnamon gum he'd been chewing in the truck and something so familiar it made her ache. It was the comfort of their history, mixed with the promise of the future.

Finally.

After all these years.

A moment ago she had been worried about all the other women, and now he was kissing her so thoroughly she just might let herself believe they could have a second chance. The feelings that had stirred when she saw him standing in the doorway of the Campbell Wedding Barn were fully awake now. And they just might consume her if she let them.

Juliette had no idea how much time had passed when they finally broke apart. It was even better than she remembered. Because they weren't kids anymore. They weren't hiding out, stealing moments. This was Jude, holding her close, kissing her lips, rendering the lost years irrelevant.

"There's so much we left undone." He rested his forehead against hers. His lips were a whisper away. "What are we going to do about it?"

How had things gone so wrong? It was hard to remember.

That was the burning question, and it brought her back to earth with a thud. It made her feel a little hollow inside. They'd once meant so much to each other, but after they'd broken up, it had seemed really and truly over. They hadn't spoken in years, yet mere hours after they'd seen each other…here they were.

She knew what she wanted, what she needed. But who knew how long he was staying. They needed to talk about things, about what happened. No matter how good things felt in this moment, they couldn't just bury the past and pretend what happened didn't happen. But she didn't know how much of the dark side of their past she wanted to dredge up right now.

Chapter Three

Kissing Jude had been like stepping back in time. They were eighteen again. They had no worries. As always, when they were together, the rest of the world didn't exist. But forty-five minutes later, Juliette was back at her house. Jude had dropped her off at the Campbell Wedding Barn where she'd left her car. She hadn't meant to make the goodbye so awkward, but Zane's truck was parked next to Lucy's house, which meant Zane and Lucy were back from their day out. If Lucy saw her climbing out of Jude's truck, her friend would have bombarded them with questions she didn't know how to answer right now. Plus, one look at herself in the rearview mirror had revealed mussed hair, kiss-swollen lips and telltale traces of the makeup she'd applied this morning. It was most definitely a post-kissing face.

Yes, one look at her and Lucy would have twigged to the situation like a divining rod. So, Juliette had gathered her purse, given Jude a quick peck on the lips, and beelined for her car before that could happen and the awkward *what's next?* conversation could present itself.

As she pulled out of the parking lot, Jude had looked a little bewildered. He'd caught her eye and put his thumb to his ear and his pinky to his mouth, making the international *I'll call you* sign.

Juliette just waved as if she hadn't noticed.

Ugh. Of course she'd noticed. But she had no idea what to do next—what she wanted or whether or not it was a good idea to even let herself go there, to let herself hope. Of course, it wasn't a good idea. Common sense dictated as much, but it seemed her heart wasn't getting the memo that reminded her that this wasn't her first Jude Campbell rodeo, and the sponsor of this one was *heartache*.

As if that wasn't enough, she had more pressing matters to contend with. Her mother's and Chelsea's cars were parked in the driveway, forcing Juliette to park in the street and do her best to get rid of the mascara smudges under her eyes. Suddenly, she was reduced to feeling like a teenager again, sneaking in after she and Jude had stolen a forbidden afternoon together. She was mortified at the prospect of facing her mother, who had never been a fan of Jude Campbell. In fact, she'd done everything in her power to throw monkey wrenches and scholarships into the path of her relationship with Jude.

What in the world were her mother and Chelsea doing here? Of course, her mother never waited for an invitation. That was Guinevere. As Juliette unlocked the door and pushed it open, she steeled herself for whatever crisis or drama or any number of other situations had enticed Guinevere out of her ivory tower.

Before she could clear the foyer, her little corgi, Franklin, came bounding around the corner, skidding on the hardwood as he barked his greeting. Juliette bent down and gave him some strokes. "Some watchdog you are, Franklin. You're supposed to keep people out, not invite them in."

The little dog rolled over on his back so she could scratch his belly. "You're hopeless. Thank goodness you're so cute." She stood up again and called, "Hello?"

"Hello?" Guinevere answered. "Juliette, darling? Is that you? We are in the kitchen. Join us, please."

Juliette was tempted to thank her mother for the invitation to enter her own kitchen, but she didn't feel like sparring. What she wanted to do was sink into a nice hot bubble bath and replay the afternoon with Jude in her head. But when she walked into the kitchen, her mother was sitting at the kitchen table with dozens of fabric swatches in front of her, sipping something from a teacup as Chelsea stood, holding up different fabric combinations, comparing them to one another. Guinevere would offer yes or no verdicts and Chelsea, who was an interior designer, would deposit them into the corresponding piles.

"Ah, there you are," Guinevere said when she saw Juliette. "I'm so glad you're home. I desperately need your expert advice. But, oh, Juliette, Chelsea is such a dear. She has agreed to help me choose the fabric for the new house. When Chelsea told me she was available to meet this afternoon, I tried to call you, but you weren't picking up. Where were you, darling?"

Juliette's gaze locked with Chelsea's, whose eyes widened as if she could read Juliette's mind, before her expression settled into a knowing smirk. Juliette tried to telegraph back, *I'll tell you everything later.* She looked away before she could ascertain whether or not Chelsea had gotten the message.

She needed to appear as normal as possible so that her mother didn't pick up on anything. As a general rule, Guinevere didn't pick up on nonverbal cues very often, but just when Juliette started to write her off as obtuse, her mother would surprise her.

"I had to meet a client at the Campbell Wedding Barn."

It was the truth.

Guinevere blanched. "And you went out of the house like that? I wouldn't call that business attire."

Juliette resisted the urge to grind her teeth. "It's Saturday, Mother. A rare Saturday that I don't have a wedding on the books. I have a day off. I had not intended on meeting with the client today, but she had an emergency. This is Saturday business casual."

Maybe the slight edge of indignation would throw Guinevere off the scent.

"Yes, well, you might want to make sure you fix yourself up before you leave the house in the future. Did you hear that Jude Campbell is home?"

Damn that betraying blush. Juliette wanted to shake herself. She'd never been one to get embarrassed easily—

certainly not one to blush like a crushing schoolgirl. If she wasn't careful she was going to tell on herself.

"Oh, really?" she said. "When did he get back?"

Chelsea gave her the side-eye.

Guinevere sniffed. "I'm not sure. You know he never was my favorite. Do you know Jude Campbell, Chelsea?"

"Mom, Chelsea is married to Jude's brother, Ethan. You know that."

Guinevere waved away the question. "Of course she is. Silly me. But, Chelsea, I'll bet you didn't know that Jude tried to talk my Juliette into giving up her scholarship."

"Mom. Really? Let's not rehash that now, okay?"

In fact, let's not rehash that ever.

"But, no, my girl was too smart and strong to be manipulated like that."

"Oh, my." Chelsea's crisp, proper British accent hid the sardonic undertone, but Juliette recognized it. "Jude is a handsome guy. That *was* strong of you, Jules."

Or stupid.

No, not stupid. She would've given up her scholarship and it would've never worked. They would've never worked.

Things happened for a reason.

"He wanted her to follow him, to go on the road with him to all those bull riding events." Guinevere looked as if she smelled something unsavory. "It would've been a disaster. A complete and utter disaster. My daughter deserves so much more. No offense to you, Chelsea.

Ethan is a fine man. In fact, I was very happy to hear he's running for mayor."

The current beloved mayor of Celebration, Ed Rosen, had been in office for nearly two decades and was retiring. Ethan was favored to be his successor.

"Ethan has my vote," Guinevere continued. "But that brother of his…"

Guinevere shook her head. Juliette gave her a piercing look.

"Mom, let's not—"

"You do know he's the world champion?" Chelsea said.

"Is he now?" Guinevere appeared unimpressed.

"And you know that world champion bull riders can win a lot of money," Chelsea persisted.

"Good for him," Guinevere said. "I didn't realize bull fighting was so lucrative. Grizzly sport—if you can even call it a sport. Poor bulls."

"He's not a bull *fighter*, Mom. He's a bull rider. Big difference. No bulls are harmed."

Guinevere rolled her eyes. "Even so, it sounds uncivilized. I suppose he's home for that big class reunion of yours?"

"I have no idea," Juliette said. It wasn't really a lie. She didn't know whether Jude was going to go to the trouble to call Marilyn Harding and ask if he could participate in the homecoming events.

She could still feel his kiss on her lips…his hands on her body… Even thinking about him and how well their bodies had worked together made her lady parts respond.

"Did you come all the way over here to grill me about Jude Campbell, Mom?"

"No. I did not." Guinevere sighed. Juliette knew her mother well enough to recognize it was a cue to ask her what was wrong. Of course she cared if something was wrong, but she was also happy for the diversion. All the better to change the subject and turn everyone's attention away from Jude and onto something else.

"Is everything okay, Mom?"

"Everything is fine." Guinevere heaved another dramatic sigh. "I suppose. I hope. Okay, I'm not sure everything is fine. Howard has been in such a cranky mood lately, snapping at me about the house, about my spending habits. He knew what he was getting himself into when he married me. I like to shop. I like nice things. After five years of marriage, it's not fair to change the rules. He was fairly warned that I am an expensive woman. He knew that before he married me. I'm afraid he's going to cut off the budget for decorating the new house. And that's all we talk about when he's at home. Most of the time lately, he isn't home."

Juliette took a cup from the cabinet and poured herself some tea from the pot her mother and Chelsea had been sharing.

"Have you sat down and talked to him about it?" she asked.

"No. I just said he's been away from the house more than he's been home," Guinevere mused. "Are you listening to me?"

"Of course I am."

"Well, I simply don't know what to make of it."

Guinevere picked up a fabric sample from one of the piles and studied it.

"I'm sure if you asked—showed him that you care—he would make time to talk to you. Communication is key in any good relationship."

Howard Albright was her mother's fifth husband. Besides Guinevere's marriage to Juliette's father, her marriage to Howard was the longest of all her marriages. Howard was a true stand-up guy. Even though Juliette loved her mother, she knew Guinevere could be a pistol at times. Poor, good-natured Howard was only human.

With a flick of her wrist, Guinevere tossed aside the piece of fabric. "I'm sure it is, but it also opens the door for talks about budget. I'm too far into decorating this house to change my plan now. I'm afraid that's what he wants to do."

"Howard is a good man," Juliette said. "Since you've been married, he has never denied you anything. In fact, he has been quite generous. If he's acting odd, you need to talk to him. People don't just start acting out of character without reason."

Guinevere stared at the large diamond on her pretty, manicured hand. Juliette could tell that her mother had something else on her mind. So she waited, hoping the silence would smoke it out.

"I guess I'm still a little gun-shy after discovering that Jerry cheated."

Jerry was husband number two. His infidelity had come as a surprise to everyone. In her late fifties, Guinevere was an attractive woman. She took care of herself. She had a figure that some thirty-year-olds would envy. She wore her sable-brown hair in a neat, stylish, age-appropriate bob. She wore just enough makeup to accentuate her sky blue eyes, but not so much that she looked like she was trying too hard. Jerry wanted an age-appropriate trophy wife and he'd gotten exactly that in Guinevere.

Trouble started in paradise when opinion-conscious Jerry decided that he did not want his wife to work and persuaded Guinevere to sell her antiques store, Little Shop of Hoarders. Lydia Clark, whose family owned the Inn at Celebration, had bought the shop. Jerry had let Guinevere keep the proceeds from the sale, but it had been the beginning of the end for their relationship. Within six months, Jerry, who owned a car dealership that was located between Celebration and Dallas, had started working more and more, putting in long hours and finding excuses to go out of town—mostly on weekends.

If Howard was changing his work habits, Juliette understood why her mother might be worried, though she had a hard time believing good old Howard would have an affair. He adored Guinevere.

"I have considered hiring a private detective to follow him," Guinevere said resolutely.

Juliette stole a quick glance at Chelsea, who had busied herself, head down, sorting an additional lot of fabric samples into piles. If Guinevere didn't mind talking about such a personal matter in front of Chelsea, it was her choice. Besides, Chelsea was trustworthy. Obviously, since that knowing look of Chelsea's suggested she might know more about with whom Juliette had spent the afternoon than she was letting on.

They'd talk about it later. That was a given.

"Mom, please don't do anything hasty until you talk to Howard. Imagine how you would feel if Howard was worried that something was wrong with you and didn't talk to you about it. I will choose to believe my stepfather is a good man until we have hard proof that he isn't."

Guinevere *harrumphed.* "Hence the need for the private investigator."

"Which you might discover you do not need if you would just talk to your husband. Howard is not Jerry. I understand the whole 'once bitten, twice shy' thing, but please talk to your husband before you jump to conclusions."

Guinevere inhaled a deep, long-suffering breath— probably giving herself time to justify her defensiveness—but her cell phone, which was lying on the table next to her, rang. Her mother grabbed it and jabbed at the connect button.

"Howard, where are you? I have been worried sick. I had to come all the way over to Juliette's just to calm down."

Phone pressed to her ear, Guinevere left the room. When they could hear that she was safely in the next room, engaging in an animated conversation with Howard, Chelsea said, "I hear you spent the afternoon with someone special?"

Juliette's hand fluttered to her neck. "Where did you hear this?"

Chelsea smiled. "Ethan was downtown earlier this afternoon doing some things for the campaign. Somebody, I can't remember who he said it was, saw you at the Redbird Diner with Jude. Is it true?"

My, oh, my, good gossip travels fast.

"Maybe."

Chelsea laughed. "Either you were there or you weren't. There is no maybe."

"Okay, Yoda. Guilty as charged."

Chelsea's eyebrows shot up. "And rumor also has it that the two of you left the diner together?"

"Yes, we did exit through the same door—the only door, besides the emergency exit, that lets people in and out of the Redbird. What's so scandalous about that?"

"You're the one who brought up the idea of *scandalous*. Methinks thou protest too much. What's going on between the two of you?"

"Nothing. There is absolutely nothing going on between Jude and me."

Juliette stood to take her mother's teacup to the sink, but she saw Chelsea hold up her hands. "If you say so, Jules. Not that there would be anything wrong if there was something between the two of you. In fact, I think it would be nice. You and I could be sisters-in-law."

The thought of marrying Jude made Juliette's heart perform a little stutter step and clinch.

She knew she was being awfully defensive, even she could see it. But the truth was, when it came to Jude, she was vulnerable. Her feelings for him could be so easily resuscitated. He was the one person in this world who could hurt her. She knew that from experience. She also knew that the two of them had lived a decade's worth of separate lives. Lives that didn't include each other. He was only here for a couple of weeks and if she knew what was best for her, they would not have a repeat performance of what happened today.

"Obviously, a change of subject is in order," Chelsea said. "My sister, Tori, is coming for a visit in a few days. She would love to pick your wedding consultant brain. She's considering opening a bridal division of Tori Ashford Alden Designs."

God love Chelsea. She was the best friend any woman could dream of. Case in point was that she knew just when to change the subject and not press the issue. Juliette would probably end up spilling everything to Chelsea sooner or later. But right now it was too raw.

"You tell her I would *love* to see her and I am happy to share everything I know."

Juliette's text tone sounded. She walked back to the table and pulled her phone out of her purse.

The text was from a woman named Marcy Johnson who worked at the courthouse and was co-chairing the homecoming festivities committee with Marilyn Harding. Juliette had known both of them since high school. In fact, all three of them had been cheerleaders together, but they traveled in different social circles now. Marcy had gotten married right out of high school. She'd married a guy from Dallas and they'd had a child within the first year of their marriage. They'd divorced a couple of years ago. A few times when Juliette had come into the courthouse with clients who had needed help with their marriage licenses—they usually needed something expedited—Marcy had helped, but they always had to endure her half-serious jokes about the perils of marriage. Her favorite one was to say that it was not too late to back out.

Even the thought made Juliette cringe.

The text said:

Are you and Jude Campbell dating again? Someone told me they saw you canoodling at the Redbird today. Everyone thought he wouldn't be able to make it back for the reunion. But since he is back, we have a whole new plan for homecoming. I'll fill you in at the meeting tomorrow. You're going to be there, right? It's at the high school at 5:45—in the library. I think you'll love it. In the meantime, bring Jude. And will you ask him to sign an autograph for my son, please? I'll owe you big-time. My boy's name is Todd.

Chapter Four

"Hey, thanks for letting me come and speak to your rodeo club," Jude said to the teens, who'd been a great audience. He'd been at Celebration High School addressing the club for more than two and a half hours. It was nearly 5:30 p.m. He'd been trying to wrap up the talk for the past twenty minutes, but the kids had so many enthusiastic questions, he hated to cut off anyone.

"It was my pleasure to be here today. But I have to scoot to another meeting here at the school library. They're trying to rope me into taking part in the homecoming festivities. I need to go make sure they don't volunteer me for something. Know what I mean?"

Everyone laughed.

Since today was more of a Q&A about his experience as a champion professional bull rider, he and the kids had met outside on the grassy area between the school's gymnasium and the library. It was such a beautiful fall afternoon, and since the kids had been cooped up in classes all day, he'd wanted to bring them outside and they'd seemed all the happier for it.

Now, in the distance, hc saw Juliette walking from the parking lot toward the library.

He was glad he'd grabbed her phone and entered his number on the way home yesterday when they were at a stoplight. She'd texted him last night saying that Marcy Johnson, a former classmate and one of the reunion committee chairs, had asked her to invite him to the meeting. He'd said he'd be there—and the timing couldn't have been better because of how it stacked up with the rodeo club meeting—but he hadn't pressed her about when he could see her again outside of the meeting. She'd seemed a little skittish when he'd left her at her car. He'd wanted to give her some room to sort things out.

A teenage girl raised her hand. She blushed when Jude nodded to her. "Do you have a date for the homecoming dance?"

Jude flashed a smile, his gaze trailing back to Juliette. "As a matter of fact, I do."

The girl looked crestfallen for a moment, but then she asked, "Who is it?"

Juliette was closer now. Jude watched her put her hand on the library door and pull it open.

"I can't say just yet. I still have to ask her."

"What if she says no?" the girl said. "Can I be your date?"

"You're too pretty to go to the dance with an old man like me," he said. "Besides, I'll bet there are plenty of guys your own age lining up to be your date."

The girl shook her head. "No one has asked me to the dance."

"Really?" said a tall, gangly boy. "I thought you already had a date. I thought you were going with Victor Hodges."

The girl shook her head again and shrugged. "No, he's taking Vanessa O'Brien."

"I'll take you to the dance," the boy said. "Do you want to go with me?"

The girl's eyes lit up and she blushed a pretty shade of pink. "Sure."

As if sensing Juliette's gaze on him, Jude glanced over and saw her watching him. Her hand was still on the door, holding it open. Their eyes locked. Jude held up his hand. She smiled and quickly slipped inside, as if she'd been embarrassed that he'd seen her watching him.

"I need to go," he said to the kids who were still there, but by this time most of them had split into smaller groups and were talking to each other or texting. The couple who had made a date for the dance had their phones out and seemed to be exchanging numbers.

Jude's work there was done. Now it was time to go secure his own date. The meeting would start in five minutes or so. If he headed in there now, he might be able to score a seat next to Juliette.

When he entered the library, it looked smaller than he remembered. The place, with its tall shelves, book smells and rows of wooden tables, had always seemed a little unnerving and unwelcoming to him. It had been the place he'd been forced to go for standardized tests and to research term papers. A couple of times, he'd even served out detention at the austere wooden tables. When he was in school, he hadn't been the studious type. His junior year, he'd been diagnosed with dyslexia after struggling with grades and, some would say, an attitude problem. It had been a relief to know there was a reason for the difficulty he'd experienced trying to focus on things that seemed to come so easily to others. Unfortunately, the diagnosis hadn't stopped his father from seizing every opportunity to brand him with the *stupid* label. It had taken years of being out in the world—away from Celebration, Texas, and his father—for him to realize while he might not have been an academic, he had a lot of common sense. After years of hard work and dedication, he'd proven himself to be a respectable athlete. That's why he couldn't make peace about retiring from the circuit without going out on top. Or even worse, retiring without even trying to get back on top.

The buzz of conversation stopped abruptly. Jude felt gazes shift to him. Someone whistled and the room erupted into applause. Jude stopped and glanced behind him, but no one else was there.

"There he is," said Marilyn Harding. She hadn't changed a bit since high school. Still the very persona of a cheerleader. "Celebration's very own world champion."

He should've gotten used to the recognition by now.

But in this context, it was embarrassing. He felt like a fraud. He'd only have the title for another couple of weeks and then someone new would walk away with the honor. The worst part was that he wasn't even able to defend it. He wasn't even able to try.

Jude smiled humbly and waved for them to stop. When the adulation finally died down, he said, "I thought George Clooney was trying to sneak into the meeting. Because surely I don't deserve such a welcome. But thanks, guys."

Jude's gaze swept the room, and he picked out Juliette amid the crowd of twenty or so who had gathered for the meeting. It made it worse that she'd witnessed the reception. She knew the truth about why he was home. She knew he was undeserving of the praise.

She was seated between two people they'd gone to school with. Their names were on the tip of his tongue, but he couldn't recall them.

Marilyn appeared at Jude's side. "Thanks for being here tonight, Jude. We're all so glad that you and Juliette could take time out of your busy schedules to join us *and* that you're as eager as we are to be part of the ten-year reunion."

They were eager? Was Juliette eager? If she was, he might be able to muster some enthusiasm.

"We have some fun things planned," Marilyn continued. "We can't wait to hear your thoughts because a lot of the plans directly involve you and Juliette. Shall we get started?"

Marilyn gestured to an empty seat next to the one she'd claimed. Jude sat down.

"Since our homecoming king and queen are both in attendance for the reunion, Marcy and I decided it might be nice to change the theme to Blast From the Past. Some of the things we have planned involve merging the reunion activities with the school's homecoming festivities. But we will have some special events that are just for the class of 2007. What do you all think of that?"

The meeting attendees applauded.

Marcy, who was sitting near Juliette, said, "Of course, we have the homecoming football game on Friday night and the dance is on Saturday night. But we thought we'd add some things. We've gotten permission to have a car in the homecoming parade on Friday before the football game. The school's committee voted and it was unanimous that they'd like for Jude and Juliette to be the grand marshals of the parade."

Everyone clapped, which made Jude squirm. His gaze found Juliette's and she looked a little embarrassed.

"Don't worry, kids," said Marilyn. "All that entails is riding in a convertible and waving to your adoring public."

"The timing will work nicely with the barbecue that we'd already scheduled for Friday before the game since there are a couple of hours between the parade and the football game," Marcy interjected. "Jude and Juliette, since you were our class's homecoming king and queen, the administration would love for you to join last year's royalty in the crowning of this year's king and queen. Does that work for you?"

"Now on to new business," Marilyn said before they

could answer. "It's traditional for the class that is celebrating its ten-year reunion to give the school a gift. It's a legacy thing. After talking to the administration, they indicated that the rodeo club would like to host a competition at the school next year. In honor of our most distinguished classmate—" Marilyn gestured to Jude "—we wanted to make a sizable donation to help make that a reality. We were hoping to donate upwards of a thousand dollars. The competition will bring good press to the school and to Celebration. So, it's a win-win for everyone. How does that sound?"

The crowd murmured their approval.

"We can raise that money through individual donations. Or we could hold a fund-raiser." The crowd groaned. "Now, come on," Marilyn urged. "This could be fun. Marcy and I were thinking we could reenact the senior talent show and charge admission. We could dust off our old numbers and acts and reenact them at the reunion talent show. Jude and Juliette, would y'all be willing to sing that song y'all performed together?"

Jude looked at Juliette, who looked as mortified as he felt.

The ideas sounded excruciating. Would people really pay money to watch others humiliate themselves— again? Okay, put in that light, he could see how it would be a success. But damn. He couldn't sing the first time around and his voice had probably gotten worse.

"Oh, what's the name of the song y'all sang?" Marcy snapped her fingers as if the action would ignite her memory. "What was it called?"

It must've worked because she virtually jumped out

of her seat with the recall. "Oh! Oh! I remember. It was that old Elton John and Kiki Dee song—'Don't Go Breaking My Heart.' Remember? It was adorable. Y'all won first place, didn't you?"

Yes, they had won. It had been total cheese. Jude's gaze connected with Juliette's again. She smiled and seemed to soften at the memory. Well, maybe it hadn't been that bad. But really, she wasn't up for re-creating it, was she? Singing in front of all those people? He hated being strong-armed into something like this.

"I just know everyone would love an encore performance and, of course, the proceeds from the event will benefit a very good cause." Marcy glanced back and forth between Jude and Juliette. "Y'all don't have to commit right now. Think about it. And that goes for everyone. I'll put a sign-up sheet on the reunion website and y'all can sign up there. This is going to be so much fun!"

"I will make a five-hundred-dollar donation if my brother gets up there and sings."

Jude's head swiveled in the direction of Ethan's voice. He must have just walked in because he was standing by the door with one hand on his hip, a bag in the other, looking smug.

"I will hold you to that, Ethan," Marilyn said. "Marcy, write that down. Ethan Campbell has pledged five hundred dollars. That will put us halfway to our goal."

As Marilyn and Marcy continued to outline the various committees that needed volunteers, Ethan came over and shook Jude's hand, pulling him into a slap-on-the-back hug. "Welcome home, little brother. I heard you made it back to town yesterday. Since you didn't come to see me, I thought I'd track you down."

"I was going to come see you later," Jude said. "I'm staying in the cabin."

Jude had wanted to settle in and gather some facts and figures on the potential property sale before he saw his brother. Even though he wasn't going to sell to MAG Holdings, he was considering listing it. Since his season had been cut short, his bank account was hemorrhaging money.

Even so, he had a feeling Ethan wasn't going to be very keen on the idea of him unloading some of the land that had been in their family for generations. Of course, he would give his brother first right of refusal.

"Sorry to interrupt the meeting, everyone," Ethan said. "I wanted to stop by and see if you all were planning on setting up tables for the mayoral candidates at the barbecue on Friday night? Since the election is a couple of weeks after homecoming, I thought it might be a good opportunity for the candidates to connect with the people. Kind of an informal meet and greet. I just happen to have some brand-spanking-new Ethan Campbell for Mayor buttons and brochures if anyone's interested."

Jude hadn't been aware that his brother was running for mayor. It made sense. He'd probably win and be good at it, too.

A couple of people raised their hands. Only Ethan could get away with a slick move like crashing a meeting he wasn't invited to and turning it into a campaign op. Ethan was beloved in this town—for the exact opposite reasons that Jude had been popular. Ethan had been the dependable son, the good student, the steady, rock-solid member of the community. He'd come home after their parents' accident and had assumed guardianship of Lucy. He'd turned around the family's failing Triple C horse-breeding ranch, making it a viable operation that had put Celebration, Texas, on the map. Except for a bout with alcoholism, which he'd won—and, according to Lucy, Ethan had been sober for years—he was pretty damn near perfect.

Jude, on the other hand, was the prodigal son who'd returned home too late for the father to slaughter the fatted calf. He was everything Ethan wasn't. Or maybe he should say that Ethan was everything he wasn't.

Marilyn and Marcy had their heads together, talking about something in low tones. Judging by their expressions, they weren't plotting to throw Ethan out of the meeting.

"Ethan," Marilyn said. "How would you like to be the emcee for the talent show?"

His brother's eyes flashed. "I'd be happy to." He jabbed his thumb at Jude. "So this one doesn't think he can weasel out of it, remind him the donation only stands if he and Juliette perform together, and it has to be that number they sang in high school."

"Thanks, bro," Jude said.

"Anytime."

Some things never changed. Ethan still loved to torture him in that way that big brothers liked to persecute younger brothers.

"That is such a generous offer, Ethan," Marilyn said. "What do you say, Jude and Juliette? Are you up for raising five hundred dollars for the rodeo club?"

Marcy bobbed up and down with excitement as she waited for Juliette to answer. "Oh, my gosh! I am so excited about this. Isn't everyone excited?"

Juliette was surprised by how sedate everyone seemed to be. Were they feeling just as trapped and pressured as she was? At least they weren't being put on the spot.

Juliette took a deep breath and reminded herself that Marcy was doing their class a big favor by putting so much hard work into organizing the event. She refused to let herself fall into the petty trap of inwardly rolling her eyes at the woman's overpowering effervescence. Once a cheerleader, always a cheerleader. Well, except she'd managed to curb her enthusiasm in adulthood. If the reunion organizing had been left to her, there would be no reunion.

Rather than inwardly snarking about how she wouldn't be one bit surprised if Marcy did backflips down the rows of stacks before breaking out into a cheer, Juliette made herself think of a kind, tactful way to disengage from this crazy talent show.

Okay, seeing the woman do backflips would be sort of amazing. Or humiliating for Juliette, if Marcy could still do a backflip ten years and one child later. Some days it was all Juliette could do to force herself to go to the gym.

"Will you do it, Juliette?" Marcy asked.

Until Marcy started pressuring her to sing, Juliette had been looking forward to the homecoming festivities. She'd even blocked off the long weekend, not booking any weddings, so that she could fully participate and help out wherever they needed her. She'd been looking forward to the break. But she did not want to get up and sing. Even if it was for a good cause. It wasn't just that she didn't have a good voice and had perennial stage fright, but to sing "Don't Go Breaking My Heart" with her ex-boyfriend, the one who had not just broken her heart, but had shattered it into a million tiny irreparable pieces she still hadn't been able to put back together, was more than ironic—it bordered on dark satire.

She couldn't figure out if Marilyn and Marcy were heartless or clueless. Maybe a little of both.

Was it too late to book herself a wedding to coordinate that weekend? She'd rather deal with the worst bridezilla than subject herself to this.

She hadn't sung in front of an audience in a decade. In fact, that talent show had been her first and last public performance. And even then, it was meant to be a joke—a means for Jude and her to poke fun at themselves.

They'd been good at that back then. They hadn't taken themselves too seriously. They hadn't taken much of anything seriously. Love had come so naturally. There had been no need to analyze it or worry about it. The fact that they could ham their way through a cornball song like "Don't Go Breaking My Heart" said it all. They'd been solid. Their relationship had seemed like a strong, unending circle that had no beginning, no ending, because love conquered all.

Ah, to be that young and naive again.

"Juliette, you wouldn't want to cost us five hundred dollars, would you?" Marcy pressed. Juliette wanted to kick her in the shin.

She felt the weight of every eye in the room on her. She couldn't look at Jude.

"How about if I make a nice donation instead?" she asked. "I'm not much of a singer. People would probably donate even more if you promised I *wouldn't* sing."

"Oh, come on and be a sport. At least you can hold a tune. You guys won, didn't you?"

They'd won because back in the day she and Jude had won everything—cutest couple, most likely to be married at the ten-year reunion, to name a few.

Now they were none of that. And she couldn't even say she'd moved on and was satisfied with her life. Over the past ten years, she'd managed to get stuck on the hamster wheel of an unfulfilling job and have a handful of relationships that had only lasted six to nine months because she was too busy working.

Not to mention, she hated being pressured like this.

"I think we'll pass," Jude said. Juliette finally looked at him. If she'd been sitting next to him, she would've hugged him.

When she glanced back at Marcy, the woman looked crestfallen. "Okay, then."

"Well, for everyone *else*, the talent show will be in the gymnasium," Marilyn said. "Anyone who wants to practice on the stage is welcome to do so. Marcy and I will be in touch with those of you who do sign up and let you know dress rehearsal times. Let us know if you have any specific needs for your act."

A sense of humor? A chastity belt? A lobotomy?

No. She would not let herself be bullied into doing something she wasn't comfortable with.

The rest of the meeting went by in a haze of *blah blah blah parade, blah blah blah barbecue, blah blah blah football game, blah blah blah dinner dance at the Campbell Wedding Barn.*

That was right. Juliette had forgotten that Lucy had mentioned they were having the reunion dance at her venue. Well, that answered her question about inventing a work engagement. She could always go out of town…

"I still need volunteers to help decorate for the dance," said Marilyn. "Marcy has the sign-up sheet over there. Lucy Campbell said there's no event the night before. If any of you are so inclined, we could set up a time to get together to decorate before the parade and after the football game on that Friday."

Stacy Edwards raised her hand. "Can't we get the current student government to help with the decorations?"

Marilyn shook her head. "The students won't be attending the same dance. They are having their own little get-together in the school gymnasium."

After answering a few more questions, Marilyn called the meeting adjourned.

Since Juliette felt like she'd let down the entire class, she decided the least she could do was help with the decorating. She walked over to Marcy and signed up to be on the decorating committee.

"I'm really sorry about the talent show, Marcy," Juliette said as she added her name to the decorating committee.

"I understand," Marcy said. Her tone was icy.

Juliette was just turning to leave when she nearly ran into Jude, who had stealthily appeared behind her. "Is this where I sign up for the decorating committee?"

For a moment, Juliette thought she might actually get to see Marcy do those backflips. "Jude Campbell! I am so grateful you want to help. Are you sure you have time? I mean, it's enough to have you back for the reunion."

Oh, gag.

Okay, so she was the bad guy for refusing.

The double standard was maddening. *But you know what? That's fine with me.*

As Jude scrawled his name on the line underneath Juliette's, Marcy and Marilyn gushed even more.

"This is going to be such fun," Marcy said. Juliette could virtually see the hearts and flowers dancing around her head. "Oh, and Jude?"

Was she batting her eyelashes?

"Yes?"

"Could I ask for one teensy little favor?" She raised her brows and shrugged.

This was an opportune moment to leave. She fished her keys out of her purse, hitched the bag up onto her shoulder and started toward the door. As she walked away, she heard Marcy ask Jude, "Would you sign an autograph for my son, Todd? He's a huge fan and he'd be so excited to get a personal message from you."

It was innocent enough. In fact, the little boy probably would be thrilled to get an autograph from his hero.

Huh. Jude was a little boy's hero. Who'd a thunk?

She got into her car, fastened her seat belt and sat there for a moment thinking before she started the engine.

What was wrong with her? Why was she wound so tightly? She really didn't begrudge Jude the warm welcome. And no, she wasn't jealous of all the predominantly female attention he was getting. He had always been a flirt and gorgeous and charismatic and being the spokesperson for the On-Off Shirt—well, he was the perfect person for the job.

So, what was wrong with her? Why was Jude's homecoming making her examine all her own inadequacies and vulnerabilities?

Because he still mattered to her.

Her heart squeezed.

His reappearance in her life was testing the very limits of her self-control. See, the thing about Jude Campbell was he could rekindle something without even realizing what he'd done and walk away. He'd done it before. He'd left her holding her broken heart in her hands.

And here she was ten years later, still not completely over it.

She'd gotten really good at not thinking about him when he wasn't there. Out of sight, out of mind. And then on the rare occasion when the specter of him had decided to drop in and haunt her, she was great at lying to herself about it—convincing herself that the pain was anger and he wasn't worth her anger because she had moved on.

But she hadn't really.

She'd given up love for a business she cared about only marginally more than the men she'd driven away. Here she was. Twenty-eight years old. Discontent. Disillusioned. Desperately trying not to let herself feel all the feelings that were breaking through now that he was back in town.

Someone rapped on her car window, startling her, making her jump. She blinked back an angry tear that had been threatening to break free and go rogue before she turned to see who it was.

It was Jude. Of course it was Jude.

He made a cranking motion with his hand. She rolled down the window.

"What is this?" She imitated the cranking motion he'd made.

"It means roll down your window, which you did."

"My windows are electric. They don't—" She repeated the cranking motion. Jude reached in and took her hand. He held it for a moment; neither of them said a word. The only sounds were of other people's muted conversation, car doors slamming, engines starting, tires crunching on the gravel drive.

Jude shifted his hand so that his fingers laced hers.

"Jude, I can't do this."

He didn't let go.

"Can we talk about it?" he asked. "If we can just sit

down and talk and you still don't want to see me, then I'll stay away."

She pulled her hand away, reclaiming her space so she could think clearly. "We've already *talked*, Jude. And look where that led us."

"Was it so bad?" he said. "It reminded me of how much I've missed you."

No, it wasn't bad. It was great.

"But you're only here for a few days—"

"Two weeks."

"Okay, two weeks. And then what, Jude? I can't just turn feeling on and off like you seem to be able to do."

"Who says I have an on-off switch?"

"But you're leaving. I'm not up for having a fling. Not with you, anyway. There's just too much history here."

He held up his hands, shook his head.

"We need to talk about this," he said. "I don't like to think of what happened yesterday—of kissing you—as a mistake, but if I'd known it would cause you any pain, I wouldn't have done it. The last thing I want to do is hurt you, Jules."

Being with him again made her feel like a compass and he was north. Since they'd been apart, she'd been traveling all kinds of twists and turns and bends in life's road trying to get herself back on the right path, but here was life, pointing her back to him.

What was she supposed to do when her true north disappeared again?

Yesterday wasn't his fault. She should've been in control. She should've never gone to the cabin with him because she'd known it would make her too vulnerable. She just hadn't thought past the moment to the aftermath of feelings. What had happened between them yesterday was proof that she couldn't trust herself with him. Admitting it to herself made her feel weak, but if she didn't face it now, she'd be up for a heap of heartache after he left.

"Let's start over," Jude said. "Let's back up and go out to dinner and get to know each other again without rushing into anything."

She shook her head.

"Think about it," he said. "Tomorrow night at seven o'clock I'll be at Café St. Germaine. If you want to talk—and only talk, just as friends—meet me there. You drive your car. I'll drive my car. No strings attached. We go home separately. Even if you beg me, I won't go home with you. Not even if you get me drunk and promise to take advantage of me."

She smiled, even against her will.

"If you don't show up, I promise I'll leave you alone."

Chapter Five

The next evening, Jude got to Café St. Germaine ten minutes early. The hostess seated him right away. He hadn't been this nervous since his last ride in the world championship. But tonight seemed more unpredictable than the fiercest bucking bull.

He rarely gave much thought to what he wore, but today he'd changed clothes three times. The first try, blue jeans and a plaid button-down, was too casual. A suit and tie that he'd tried on in a Dallas department store was too formal. He'd struck a happy medium with a pair of khakis and a new white polo shirt. He'd even gotten a haircut for the occasion.

He'd needed one. His hair was too long and he justified the khakis because obviously he didn't have anything that could pass for *upscale casual*, as the guy in the men's department had called it. Until today, upscale casual hadn't even been part of his vocabulary.

He felt naked without his hat, but even he knew it had no place tonight. His boots did, though. They kept him grounded. He'd cleaned them up and had given them a quick coat of polish. Now here he sat at Café St. Germaine, as antsy as he'd been when he'd wait for the chute to open and a particularly important ride to begin.

The analogy applied here. Waiting here for Juliette, it could be the beginning of a good ride. Or if she decided not to show he would have to pick himself up and deal with the pain and disappointment. But at least he would know where they stood. This was the first step toward seeing if there was still anything between them.

Or if he should move on.

Moving on sounded good in theory, but time had proven, with Juliette, it was easier said than done.

But it was time. It was part of his next step, but first he had to figure out what his next step would be. Which direction would this go?

He glanced at the time on his phone. Six fifty-nine. He picked up his water glass, which the server had already refilled once, and took a long sip. He had decided to wait for her to order a drink. If she didn't show, it would be a lot easier to move into the bar without a tab.

The restaurant was doing a brisk business. It wasn't overly crowded but enough people were coming and going that every time the door opened and someone who wasn't Juliette walked in his heart sank a little lower. He could always occupy himself by checking email on his phone, but there was bound to be something from his agent pushing for an answer on whether he was going to commit to next season, or from Afton with thinly veiled questions that were supposed to look like business, but edged into the margins of too personal since she was just a friend and would never be anything more. He didn't want to have any of that on his mind. Tonight, he wanted to focus on Juliette.

Then, as if he'd conjured her, the door opened and she walked in. She said something to the hostess, who pointed her in the direction of the corner table he'd asked for because it seemed relatively private, not too close to the other diners. That way, no matter what they ended up talking about, they wouldn't feel as if they were being overheard.

He watched her as she walked toward him looking effortlessly sexy in the blue dress and heels she was wearing. Her long, dark hair hung loose around her shoulders. She could've come directly from a business meeting or she might have chosen that outfit for him. It didn't matter. She was here. And she was smiling at him as she approached.

He stood up, fueled by the nervousness he thought would go away as soon as she arrived. But it was still sticking around like an interloper.

"You made it."

Even though tonight was supposed to be about friendship, about no strings attached, it was perfectly natural to enfold her in a hug and kiss her on the cheek. She hugged him back, which was a good sign, but he wasn't going to read anything into it.

"Of course. I had to come," she said. "If I hadn't,

when were we going to plan our strategy to convince Ethan to make that five-hundred-dollar donation, even though we're not performing?"

"I am so glad you didn't want to do that duet," Jude said as he pulled out her chair and helped her scoot closer to the table. And just like that, they fell into the same ease and comfort that had always defined them.

"I couldn't sing back then and I know I haven't gotten any better," he said. "Only this time people would know what to expect so they'd probably come armed with rotten tomatoes. It was bound not to end well, no matter what happened. Bad singing. Rotten tomatoes. Both?"

She threw her head back and laughed. The sound pierced him all the way through to his soul. It would have seemed so natural to reach out and take her hand. Instead, he fisted his into the tablecloth that was bunched up around his knees.

"What's going on with the property sale?" she asked. "Have you talked to Ethan about it yet?"

He shook his head. "You heard him last night. We haven't even had a chance to see each other."

Juliette nudged his arm. "Then what are you doing here with me tonight? You should be with your brother. You two have a lot to talk about."

"Don't worry. I have my priorities straight."

Her expression was a question mark.

Juliette glanced down at her hands. Then she brushed invisible crumbs off the tablecloth.

The server came and went over the specials. Jude ordered a glass of chardonnay for Juliette and a beer for himself. After he left, they quietly perused the menus.

"I'm not selling to MAG Holdings," he said. "My brother won't be happy when he finds out I want to list the property, but selling it to a developer would have spelled family feud for sure."

"So, you're still planning on selling the place?" she said as she closed her menu and set it to the side.

Jude shrugged. "I don't know yet. But what I do know is that all we've done since I've been home is talk about me. Why do you keep deflecting when I ask about you?"

Juliette shrugged. "I don't like to talk about myself."

Jude laughed. "Yet you expect me to spill it all. I seem to remember someone saying, 'Tell me everything.'"

"And I don't think you finished, did you?" she said.

"It's your turn now," he said. "So, tell me everything."

"Everything?" she asked. "I seem to remember someone saying everything was a tall order."

They laughed at the way the conversation tables had turned. The server returned with their drinks and took their orders. He ordered the filet, medium rare. She ordered the salmon.

"Everything," Jude reminded. "I want to know about you."

"You know me, Jude. I'm the same person. What you see is what you get."

He loved what he saw.

"What have you been doing all these years?"

"Where do I even start?"

"Start at the beginning. I guess you can skip over the part about all the Euro princes you met in college."

"There were no Euro princes."

"Chelsea didn't try to fix you up with the guys in her circle?"

His sister-in-law, Chelsea, had relocated to Celebration, Texas, from London. She was some kind of British noblewoman, though Jude didn't know exactly what kind. She'd been Juliette's college roommate. She'd met his brother, Ethan, when she'd come to visit Juliette in Texas. She'd been running from a scandal—though Jude never figured out what all the hubbub had been about. Aside from her accent—and the fact that her brother was the United Kingdom's new prime minister—people would never guess she came from such a highbrow background.

"Never mind, I don't want to know about the guys. But I am curious, after all the time you spent in Europe, how did you end up back in Celebration?"

"Don't be dissing your hometown, Campbell. Celebration is a pretty cool spot. A lot of people have gone away and chosen to come back."

"Who says I'm dissing it? I'm back, aren't I?"

"Are you back?"

He shrugged. "I don't know how long I'll stay, but I'm here now."

Something sensual passed between them. The feeling knocked him for a loop and had him scrambling to get back on neutral ground so that he could keep his promise that tonight they would talk—and only talk— just as friends.

"It sounds like your business is booming," he said. "How did you get into the wedding planning business?"

Her eyes widened. "I thought you hadn't kept tabs on me."

He shrugged. "Lucy kept me informed. You know she always wanted us to end up together. So, she has gone out of her way to keep me up on all things Juliette."

Juliette grimaced. "Lucy hasn't been quite so forthcoming with me about info pertaining to you."

"What can I say? She's my sister. She's loyal."

"Then again," Juliette said. "Lucy hasn't been back in Celebration very long. She's been busy with Zane and establishing her own business."

His sister was another one who had gone away only to find herself drawn back to her hometown after searching for herself elsewhere.

"If you already know everything, why do I need to tell you?" Juliette asked.

Jude reached out and brushed a strand of hair off her forehead. "Because I'm sure Lucy didn't tell me *everything*, and I want to know everything. Everything."

The look on her face was so vulnerable it made his heart squeeze. That's when the server chose to deliver the food, spoiling the moment. Or maybe saving them. It was hard to tell.

Once they had settled in again, he said, "You were getting ready to tell me, how was it that you ended up back in Celebration?"

She chewed her food for a moment and then swallowed. "I hadn't intended to stay. I came home for Mom's wedding. Her fifth wedding."

She pursed her lips and gave Jude a knowing look.

"No, actually, this guy, Howard, that's husband number five's name, he's good for her. I think of all her relationships besides her marriage to my dad, this one might stick."

Jude nodded. "Good for Guinevere. What happened to husbands two, three and four?"

"Yeah, that will take a while."

"I'm all yours."

"Okay, you asked for it." She set down her knife and fork, picked up her wine, and took a fortifying sip. "Number two's name was Jerry." Juliette grimaced. "Good ol' Jerry turned out not to be such a good guy after all. He wore her down until she agreed to sell her business."

She regaled him with the story.

Jude's jaw dropped. "Thinking about Guinevere without the Little Shop of Hoarders is just weird. That place was her pride and joy."

"Yes. But Jerry didn't want his wife to work. I guess he saw it as some sort of status symbol to have a wife who solely catered to him. The shop and all of those overseas antique-buying trips took up a lot of her time and attention, took it away from him. He didn't like to travel. So she would go alone. Then, probably six months after she sold the shop, she discovered Jerry was having an affair with his administrative assistant. I guess he didn't think things through very well. Every time Mom would go out of town on a buying trip, he would hook up with his mistress. But after she sold the shop, there were no more buying trips. He was pretty cocky to think he could continue his business as usual after he had Mom at his beck and call. Obviously, he didn't know Guinevere very well. She's like a bloodhound—with all due respect to my mother. Once she gets a scent of something that doesn't smell right, she won't stop until she roots it out. It didn't take long for her to realize something was up with Jerry and his bimbo, as she called her."

Jude frowned. "What a bastard."

"Oh, wait, it gets better with number three—or maybe I should say it's worse, depending on how you look at it. But first, you'll never guess what number three's name was. Take a guess."

He gave her the side-eye. "I have no idea. What?"

"*Lance*. Guinevere thought she'd finally found her Lancelot."

"Get out." He laughed. "What happened to Lancelot?"

"Lancelot—er, Lance—was about fifteen years younger than Guinevere."

Jude's eyebrows shot up. "Go, Guinevere."

Juliette shook her head. "Lance was no knight in shining armor. He ended up stealing all the money she'd gotten when she sold Little Shop of Hoarders. I mean, at least Jerry had the decency to let her keep the proceeds from the sale. This guy stole from her."

She went on to detail how husband number four ended up being a control freak. "She had to threaten him with a restraining order, but finally he got the picture and granted her a divorce. That marriage was so messy I was tempted to think of her marriage to Howard as a rebound. You know, someone to make her feel safe and adored. Because Howard absolutely adores her. But I think the fifth time is the charm. I hope, anyway. The sad thing is, until Howard, it seemed like she had to give up so much of herself for love."

"That's a shame," Jude said. "But not with Howard, right? I mean, when love is right you shouldn't feel like you're giving up anything."

Juliette shrugged and changed the subject to her business.

She answered some questions about it. The most extravagant wedding she'd planned: the budget was a quarter of a million dollars; an intimate affair for five hundred people; the bride's dress cost fifty thousand dollars; they hired an entire symphony orchestra to perform during the reception.

A couple of her weddings had been featured in national magazines. "For a while, travel was a nice perk, but after a while, living out of a suitcase four and five days a week starts to become a strain.

"It's hard, because I have a dog now. Did I tell you I have a dog?" Her eyes lit up and she looked a lot happier than she had when she was telling him about the daily grind of her business.

He smiled and shook his head.

"But Lucy told you, didn't she?"

He swallowed the last bite of his steak. "She might've mentioned it. A corgi, right?"

Her brows shot up. "You get extra points if you know his name."

"Franklin."

Her mouth fell open. She leaned back in her chair

and crossed her arms. "I'm sensing an unfair advantage here. And I'm also wondering why I talked all the way through dinner if you already knew all this. I mean, I guess I should be flattered that you cared enough to keep up with me all these years—and to hear it again." She laughed.

He hoped it didn't sound stalker-ish. His sister loved to talk and when it came to any information about Juliette, he loved to listen. It had been like offering a starving man a feast.

The server appeared again to clear the plates and ask if they wanted dessert—they didn't; they were too full.

Between the time it took for Jude to pay the bill and for them to leave the restaurant and start walking to their cars, Juliette had become a little quieter and more subdued than she had been before he'd tipped his hand and told her he had indeed kept tabs on her all these years. He wasn't going to lie.

"Are you okay?" he asked.

Her smile was a little too bright. "I'm fine. I'm great. I enjoyed dinner. Thank you. My car is right over here."

She hooked her thumb in the direction of a row of cars parallel parked on Main Street. Within a few steps, they were standing by her Prius.

He intended to keep his promise. No pressure. No good-night kiss, even though he was dying to revisit what they had started that first day at the cabin. But he'd promised he would mind his manners and he sensed that she was feeling a little overwhelmed after learning about his reconnaissance.

"Can we do this again? Soon?" he asked.

She was looking down, fishing her keys out of her purse. When she looked up her eyes were so heartbreakingly earnest, it knocked him for a loop.

"What are we doing, Jude? I mean, what do you want? From me?" Her hand fluttered to her neck in a nervous gesture. "From us?"

He didn't quite know how to answer that. Not yet. That's what he was hoping to figure out while he was home. He needed to know if they were on the same page, wanted the same things—

"It's taken me a long time to get over you." She squeezed her eyes shut. "I told myself I wasn't going to say that. It's not your problem. It's mine. But I'm fine now. Really, I am."

"Are you?" he asked.

"Of course."

"Are you completely over me, Juliette? Have you moved on?"

"Jude, you really did a number on me."

"You're the one who turned down my proposal," he said. "I mean, since we're laying it all out on the table. I wanted to marry you."

"And then three months later you come back for Christmas engaged to someone else."

"I didn't marry her."

"Do you know that I came back that Christmas ready to give up everything for you? Scotland, my scholarship, college. And then there you were with her. You'd moved on so seamlessly that it felt like you and I never even happened."

What? The words hit like a slap square in the face.

"You didn't come home for Christmas that year. Or any of the years after that as I recall."

"Yes, I did. Not only was I here, but I'd planned on not going back to Scotland until my mom told me you were engaged. But I didn't believe it. I was on my way over to see you, because I was sure you would tell me that everything was a mistake, a big misunderstanding. But before you saw me, I saw you with her. You were downtown. You were kissing her. I went home. Guinevere helped me change my ticket and I went back to school the very next day. I couldn't deal with the thought of running into you with someone else."

He was so stunned; he was still trying to digest what she'd said. "You were going to give up everything for me? For us?"

She nodded, but the gesture was swallowed up when she shrugged at the same time.

"I'm sorry. She ended up being just a rebound…a mistake. My parents never met her. My dad and I still hadn't made amends. I called the house to see if I could come over, but my mom said it was still too soon. It was Christmastime and my dad still couldn't put our differences behind him. But none of that matters now."

He let the words hang in the air, teetering on the emotions suspended between them.

"I've wondered for a long time if maybe things were meant to be this way." His voice was hoarse with emotion. "Maybe we've been on this crazy path because we weren't ready for each other then. We loved each other, but I don't know if we were ready for each other, for *this*… I don't know that we were ready for *us*. I'm not saying I'm glad we broke up, but going away to school in Scotland and spending time in Europe has made you who you are today and all these years I have channeled this restlessness I've always battled into riding bulls."

She crossed her arms and braced her back against the door of her car. "So where does that leave us now?"

Where did it leave them? "I want to spend time with you, Jules. Do we have to label it?"

"Don't you think your adoring public will want to know what's going on with the ex-girlfriend that you're spending so much time with?"

He raised a brow. "Oh, are we going public with this?"

"I didn't say anything about going public. I just need to know where your head is. What you want."

Fair enough.

"We're seeing each other. Trying to figure things out. Does that work for you?"

"No sex," she added, a bit too hastily for his liking.

"Not even if you get me drunk. Not even if you beg me. Well, maybe if you beg me."

He smiled at her. "I want you to feel safe with me, Jules." He put both hands on his chest. "This is a safe place. Can we give ourselves some time to figure out what's going on?"

She searched his face, his eyes. Then nodded. "Do you want to meet for lunch tomorrow?"

"I can't tomorrow. I have to go to Dallas for a meeting with my agent and sponsor. Want to ride along?"

"I have to work, Jude. I have a consultation with a potential new client."

"Okay, I understand. If something changes, let me know."

"Is this meeting about next season?"

"It is. We're going to talk about the terms of my sponsorship."

"Have you decided what to do yet?"

"Not yet. The meeting will help me get closer to making a decision. I talked to my accountant. He said if I have one more good year, I might not need to sell the property."

"But isn't there another way?"

What he didn't say was that if he bowed out now, he'd have to come up with a new plan. A new life plan. Jude had known this day was coming—he hadn't planned for it to come so soon. He had a couple of ideas about what he wanted to do, but they would take some fleshing out. Frankly, until this season had come to an abrupt end, he'd been so busy with competitions and his obligations to his sponsorship that he hadn't had time to work on much else.

They stood there in silence for a moment.

"There's always a way," he said. "Did you know the only reason I agreed to this On-Off Shirt foolishness is because a portion of the sales benefit a charity?"

Her eyes widened and she shook her head.

"Of course you didn't know that because that's not the message that Copenhagen is pushing. The image they've cultivated for me is sexy bad boy."

"Why is that a bad thing? You know you are a whole lot more than a narcissistic pretty boy. As long as you know who you are, public opinion shouldn't matter."

"Do you know who I am, who I've become over the years that we've been apart, Jules? Because I don't want you to have any misconceptions."

"Does what I think matter to you?"

He swallowed the lump in his throat. This was supposed to be a no-pressure night, but now that she'd asked he couldn't tell her anything but the truth. "Of course what you think matters. You are one of the only people—maybe the only one—whose opinion matters. I can play the game. I have played it for quite a while now, but sometimes you just get tired of pretending to be someone you're not. Know what I mean?"

He recognized the spark in her eyes. "I know exactly what you mean. I'm ready for a change, too."

"Come on the road with me," Jude said before he could stop himself.

She smiled and rolled her eyes as if he were making a joke.

"You don't think I'm serious. I'm serious. We could travel the US for a year or two and then figure out what to do next."

"The reason I know you're joking is because I know you remember how much I hate bull riding. Now that I know what the doctors have said, that you'd be going against doctors' orders to ride again, there's no way I could just stand by and watch you put yourself in danger. But you were only joking, right?"

* * *

Was Jude joking? Juliette wondered as she braked to a stop at a red light.

Surely, he was joking. Because he wouldn't believe that she would actually put her life on hold to follow him all over the country, would he?

She had made a joke out of it and had leaned in and planted a good-night kiss on his cheek. Before he could say anything else, she'd said good-night and had gotten in her car and driven away, leaving him standing on the sidewalk.

The most ridiculous part of it all was that part of her would've loved to toss everything and go off on a grand adventure, the road trip of a lifetime, just Jude and her. Without the bull riding.

But they weren't eighteen anymore and all of her dissatisfaction with her own life would still be waiting for her back home when the shine had worn off the journey. Why was it that love always seemed to come at such a great price? She'd experienced that with Jude years ago; she'd seen it with her mother and her string of husbands. Now, the only man she'd ever loved was back in town, but she could see the warning lights ahead—if she wasn't careful she would end up crashing and paying dearly with a broken heart.

It was only nine o'clock. She had too much nervous energy to go home. If she did, she would just toss and turn or eat something she wasn't supposed to. She wasn't even hungry. She was such a stress eater.

The light was still red, so she pulled her phone out of her purse and texted Chelsea.

Are you awake? I just finished having dinner with Jude and I was wondering if I could come over for some girl talk?

Yes! Come over! Please! I have a surprise for you!

Chelsea must've been drinking wine because in addition to the regiment of exclamation points, she capped off the message with a cast of emojis that included smiley faces, hearts, flowers, wineglasses—and was that a taco and zucchini? *Um...okay.*

The person in the car behind her honked. Juliette looked up to see the light had turned green and there was a lot of space in front of her where the other cars had already gone on their way. She tossed her phone onto the seat, glanced in her rearview mirror, waved her apology to the person behind her and sped off.

She arrived at Chelsea and Ethan's house about ten minutes later. Chelsea had turned on the porch light for her. She parked and made her way up the porch steps and knocked on the door.

Chelsea answered, two flutes of champagne in hand. "You're here! I'm so glad you decided to come over." She handed Juliette one of the glasses of champagne and linked her free arm with Juliette's. "Look who else is here. My sister arrived early. She's the surprise."

Pencil thin and posh as a London fashion plate, Chelsea's sister, Tori Ashford Alden, perched elegantly and languidly on the living room couch. Her blond hair was cut in a fashion-forward short do. She wore a sleek, body-hugging minidress with the most gorgeous pair of black boots that Juliette had ever seen. No doubt, the entire ensemble was from her latest Tori Ashford Alden collection.

She and Juliette greeted each other with double cheek kisses.

"Jules, your ears must have been burning," Chelsea said, "because Tori and I were talking about you right before you texted. She is dying to pick your brain. I promised her you would tell her everything you know about the American wedding industry."

Juliette was happy to see Tori. Really, she was. But she would've been lying if she hadn't admitted to herself that she felt a teensy bit disappointed that she would not be able to tell Chelsea what had transpired tonight with Jude. Back in college, her friend had always been the voice of reason. She was counting on Chelsea to help her sort out her mixed emotions. She was depending on her friend to point out what an impossible situation this was if she thought for one second that Jude Campbell wouldn't break her heart again. He was at a crossroads in his life. He was discontent and was looking for something that felt familiar...at least until he figured out what he wanted to do next. She was more convinced than ever that love always came with a cost, and she had a feeling if she let Jude in, she'd end up paying dearly.

But it was probably just as well that she and Chelsea couldn't talk right now. She'd seen Ethan's truck in the driveway. It was probably best not to talk about Jude in his brother's house. For that matter, she was probably better off giving herself time to come back down to earth and put things into perspective so that she didn't say something she'd be embarrassed about later.

The three women had just settled into champagne and girl talk when a knock sounded on the front door.

Chelsea glanced at her phone. "Good grief. It's after nine thirty. Who in the world is that?"

She answered the door and Juliette recognized the sound of Jude's voice. "I'm sorry to barge in so late. Is my brother still awake?"

"He sure is," she said. "Come in and join the party."

Chelsea appeared in the living room with her arm linked through Jude's. "Juliette, look who I found."

Chapter Six

"Are you following me?" Juliette's right brow shot up in that sassy way that always made Jude smile.

He held her gaze. "I'd follow you anywhere. The question is would you follow me?" She blushed and he hoped she was recalling their conversation they'd had before she'd sped off. He noticed that Chelsea and her sister were exchanging curious glances.

"Why do I feel as if I've stumbled into the midst of an intimate conversation?" Tori asked. One of the woman's rail-thin arms was stretched along the back of the red leather couch. A champagne glass, the stem of which was balanced between the middle and ring fingers of her upturned palm, dangled precariously, as if it might drop to the floor if she shifted her wrist.

No one answered her question.

He wondered if Juliette had thought about his offer to come with him on tour. Was that what had spurred her to come over here? If she'd join him, it would breathe new life into what felt like an arduous task.

"Don't let me interrupt," he said. "As you were. I'll go find Ethan."

"Last I knew, he was out back working in the shed," Chelsea said. "Would you like a beer?"

Jude waved her off. "Thanks, I'll get it."

Unless Chelsea had rearranged the kitchen, he knew where to find the beer and bottle opener. He, Lucy and Ethan had grown up in this house. Ethan had inherited it with his third of the property after their folks died. It was surreal finding himself back here after all these years. Everything looked the same, but at the same time, everything was completely different.

That seemed to be the theme these days. Exactly the same, but completely different. Especially with Juliette sitting in the living room. She was here, but not with him. Not this time.

He grabbed a beer and went out back, holding the screen door as it closed so it didn't slam. Their mom used to yell at them about slamming the door. Catching it before it closed was a reflex. His gut clenched at the memory.

This was the only home he'd ever known since he'd been on the road for the better part of the past decade. The ninety acres of land that comprised the Campbell Ranch had been in the family for generations. Telling Ethan that he was thinking about selling wasn't going to be an easy conversation. The only way he could soften the blow was to offer Ethan first right of refusal. There was a case to be made for his part of the land sitting vacant and dormant all these years. It's not as if he were pulling the rug out from under Ethan and selling his livelihood. Ethan had his own piece of the Campbell legacy.

The property taxes were due on November 1. It would take every spare penny that Jude could scrape together to pay them. In his championship year, he'd won a nice purse, but after sitting out a few matches—forfeiting the chance to defend his title—and paying his doctor bills, he'd almost depleted his resources.

Even though being back here excavated some challenging memories along with the sweet ones of Juliette, it was killing him to sell off his legacy, but he simply didn't have the money to hang on to it. If he sold, he would have the capital he needed to start over.

Right now, all he wanted was to start over. Start this next part of his life.

From the porch, he could see that the light was on in the shed. His boots sounded on the boards as he made his way down the porch steps. In the glow of the full moon, he could see that Ethan had given the porch a fresh coat of paint. His brother always had taken pride in the homestead. If Jude did end up selling his piece of the family history, at least Ethan, living in the house they'd grown up in and reviving the Triple C Ranch, would be the keeper of their past.

As Jude drew closer, he could hear Ethan rustling around in the shed.

"Need some help?" he said as he pulled open the door.

Ethan dropped a shovel he'd been holding. He muttered a couple of curse words under his breath as the tool clattered to the ground.

"What the hell, Jude? Don't sneak up on someone like that. You're lucky I didn't hit you with the shovel instead of dropping it."

"Sorry about that, man. I didn't know how else to announce myself. What are you doing out here at this hour?"

"I needed to get some things to bring to the stables tomorrow. I thought I would give Chelsea and Tori some time to talk."

"Yeah, Juliette's here, too."

"Did she come with you?"

Jude shook his head.

"I thought you said you two were having dinner tonight."

"We did. Then we both ended up driving over here separately."

Ethan picked up his own beer—a nonalcoholic variety—which was sitting in a koozie on the potting bench, and took a swig. Ethan had nearly reached rock bottom at one point in his battle against alcoholism, but through sheer grit and determination he'd managed to win the war. Now he didn't touch the real stuff.

"How are you two doing?" he asked.

Jude shrugged. "I can't say that there is an *us two*. It's a little early for that."

"You could've fooled me. You weren't even sitting next to each other at the meeting, but it still seemed like nothing had changed. The reunion committee even has you two performing together for the talent show."

"Yeah, we're not going to do that," Jude said. "What was your magnanimous offer about, anyway?"

"It's tradition for the class celebrating the reunion to make a donation to the school," Ethan said. "Your class is going to sell tickets to raise the money."

Jude held up his hand. "You know that's not what I'm talking about. I mean what the hell were you doing making that five-hundred-dollar donation with a contingency of Juliette and me singing?"

Ethan laughed. "What can I say? I'm a supporter of the arts."

Jude thought of several comebacks, but shelved them. He just didn't have it in him tonight to spar with his brother.

"Did you come over just to chew me out for that? Actually, I thought I was helping your cause."

Jude had a flashback to the night of his senior prom. Ethan had slipped him some condoms and in a fatherly way told him to have fun and be careful. As if he were still a virgin and prom night was the night he'd get lucky. God knew their dad had never stepped up to offer fatherly advice or protection—neither physical nor emotional. But Ethan had always been wise beyond his years. He'd just gotten home from his junior year at college. Jude hadn't had the heart to tell him that his and Juliette's virginity train had left the station a long time before prom night. He got the feeling that Ethan would somehow be disappointed in him.

That's the way he was feeling right now. That he

was going to let his brother down, let his family down, again. It's what he was dreading, the inevitable disappointment in his perfect older brother's eyes when he told him of his plans. Jude steeled himself inwardly. He should be used to it by now. Nothing that he'd done in his life had ever not disappointed someone. That's why he'd adopted the motto, *You can't please everyone. So, you might as well please yourself.*

Ethan handed Jude the shovel he'd dropped. "Help me take some stuff up to the back porch and we can sit and finish our beers."

It was a good plan. It would be easier to deliver the news in the moonlight rather than under the harsh, naked bulb in the shed. Somehow that unforgiving, stark light made what he had to say seem even worse.

Shovel in one hand and beer in the other, Jude stepped out of the shed. He heard Ethan click off the light, heard the dull rattle of the tools his brother was carrying, heard the sound of the door clicking shut behind him.

The night smelled loamy and cool-humid. The promise of fall hung in the air as they walked in silence across the lawn back to the freshly painted steps. After they'd deposited the tools onto the porch, they both settled onto a step and sat in silence for a couple of minutes.

Ethan always had been a man of few words. Jude knew he was the one who needed to drive the conversation. Hell, of course he did. If not, they'd end up sitting in companionable silence for most of the night.

Jude took one more fortifying draw from his beer and steeled his resolve.

"Did you ever think about expanding the Triple C?" Ethan had already worked hard to rebuild it to the level it had been before their father had gotten ahold of it and threatened to let it die from neglect and drunken disinterest.

"Oh, I've thought about it. It's in the five-year plan. Why do you ask?"

"Because I'm thinking of selling my land and I wanted to offer it to you first."

Ethan didn't say anything for a long while. He just sat there on the step with his elbows braced on his knees, beer bottle in one hand. Jude could see his silhouette in the moonlight as his brother stared straight ahead into the inky abyss.

Knowing Ethan the way he did, Jude knew he was digesting what he'd just said. His brother was a man of few words at the best of times. When confronted with something hard, Ethan usually retreated into his head for a while.

Jude stayed quiet, respecting that, listening to the symphony of cicadas and croaking frogs playing off in the distance.

"I don't know what you want me to say, Jude. I'm not in the position to buy your land for market value and I wouldn't expect you to sell it to me for anything less." He sounded annoyed. "Are you really that hell-bent on divesting and distancing yourself from the family? I know you and Dad had some tough times, but he's been gone a long time now, and I'd like to think that you wouldn't carry a grudge against a dead man."

It was easy for Ethan—the perfect son—to talk about not holding grudges.

"Yeah, well, I guess it's easy to judge when you're not walking in someone else's shoes."

Ethan growled an expletive.

Jude stood. "Look, I don't owe you any explanations. I came here as a courtesy to you. To let you know my plans and to offer you first right of refusal—"

Ethan frowned up at him from his place on the steps. "You know I'm not made of money. If you'd bothered to keep in touch you might know that I've invested everything I have in returning the Triple C to profitability. You can't just come in here and expect me to write a check without warning."

"I don't expect anything from you," Jude said. "If you'd get the chip off your shoulder and ask me about details rather than jumping to conclusions, maybe you'd understand that I'm not doing this just to get under your skin or to make a point. I'm not selling to distance myself from the family. I have my reasons, Ethan. Do you think I want to sell off part of our legacy? If you knew me as well as you're chiding me for not knowing you, you'd know that this is breaking me."

"Sit down." Ethan took a long draw of his beer. Jude sat.

"You're right. Tell me what's going on with you. Why are you selling the property?"

Again, Ethan stared straight ahead into the distance. It would be easier to talk to him this way. It would be best just to be straightforward. It was hard and humbling to confess how his life was kind of a hot mess, when his older brother seemed to always do everything right.

Actually, that wasn't absolutely true. Ethan had known his share of troubles. In addition to the alcoholism, his brother had been through a divorce, and of the three plots of land he, Ethan and Lucy could choose from, Ethan had chosen the one that needed the most work to make it sustainable, so that it not only met but exceeded its value. But he'd faced it all and come out the other side a winner. He was remarried to the love of his life, and even though he claimed to not have a lot of liquid assets, the Triple C was thriving. Everything his brother touched turned to gold. Maybe not immediately, but through sheer pigheadedness and a resolute resolve not to quit until he had won, Ethan Campbell never seemed to fail. It dawned on Jude that even though they were different people, maybe he could learn something from his brother.

Jude told Ethan about his injuries and how they had sidelined him.

"If I ride one more season and win, I might not have to sell," he said. "I have enough money saved to pay the property taxes and upkeep for another year, but after that I'm tapped out. If I do go another season, it will probably be my last. I'd hoped to get in two more good years on the circuit, but I'm twenty-eight years old. I've reached the end of the road. I have some ideas of what's next, but this year's injuries and setbacks pushed back my progress."

"Regardless, you're going to have to do something," Ethan said.

"I know that," Jude snapped.

Ethan held up his hand. "Have you given any thought to what you want to do?"

"Of course I have."

"Would you care to share?"

"I need to figure some things out before I talk about it. I need to figure out how to get from here to there. I have a meeting tomorrow with Copenhagen and my agent. My decision on whether to ride next year will depend on what happens in that meeting."

"You know, there's no shame in asking for help," Ethan said. His voice was less edgy now.

Jude nodded.

He knew, but knowing and doing were two different things. He didn't want to be a burden…and he hated being beholden to anyone. Especially family. His father had taught him that lesson the hard way. But there was no way in hell he was going to tell his brother that. He could already hear Ethan saying, *If you can't count on family, who can you count on?*

Jude had learned a long time ago that it was better to count on no one but himself.

The next day, Tori met Juliette at her office. They had spent a great deal of the previous night talking shop. Tori had picked Juliette's brain about every aspect of the wedding business; then she had asked if she could spend the day at the shop with her.

Of course she could. However, Tori was an internationally renowned fashion designer, and Juliette couldn't help but wonder what Tori thought she could learn from her.

Juliette had gotten to know Tori when she and Chelsea had been roommates at St Andrews. Regardless of what happened, it would be fun to spend some time with her.

While she was waiting for Tori to arrive, Juliette had rushed around, picking up her small office, which was located in a storefront on Main Street, in downtown Celebration. Since her business had grown, she had considered moving to larger digs. It would've made sense to move her operation to Dallas, but she enjoyed being in the heart of downtown Celebration. As part of the downtown merchants' association, she felt like part of the community. And she loved her shop, with its hardwood floors, whitewashed brick walls and crown molding. The storefront windows provided a lot of natural light and the place just had a good energy about it. Everything was made even more beautiful by all the wedding paraphernalia displayed around the space: bridal gown samples, veils that Juliette had designed and made herself, dinner place settings, champagne flutes, bouquets and floral centerpiece samples were displayed under strings of tiny white twinkle lights. The magical energy of the place had taken five years of hard work and determination to cultivate. Though, as she relocated the six shoe boxes that contained Tabatha Jones's freshly re-dyed lavender pumps, which now matched the bridesmaids' dresses exactly, Juliette wondered how it was that her shop's energy didn't reflect the hundreds of bridezillas who had stormed through the place over the years she'd been in business. Granted, not all of them were bridezillas, but it was safe to say that the vast majority of them had presented a challenge that sometimes crossed the line between concerned client and three-headed monster.

She would need to call Tabatha today and arrange a time to present her with the miracle she had performed. Actually, it hadn't been that difficult. Juliette had simply taken the shoes and a fabric sample that matched the dresses down the street to her friend Nora at Sassy Feet Shoe Repair.

So much for letting Tabatha suffer the consequences of going against Juliette's recommendations and ordering from Italy.

Juliette sighed. Once a people pleaser, always a people pleaser. It was her burden to carry.

She should have Tori come with her and meet Tabatha. Juliette chuckled at the mental image of Tabatha's face when she realized that the one and only Tori Ashford Alden was delivering her purple bridesmaids' shoes. It wouldn't necessarily be rewarding bad behavior as much as cultivating good karma by showing Tabatha her bad behavior hadn't ruffled her in the least.

Juliette quickly dusted two dress mannequins that showcased her own designs—actually, they weren't her originals. She had created the patterns and sewed the dresses based on sketches that Dorothy Phillips, the late mother of Lucy's fiancé, Zane, had drawn. They were part of a memorial to Dorothy that the town of Celebration had held in her honor after she passed away earlier that year. Juliette had always loved to sew and she was humbled by the chance to bring Dorothy's creations to life. The blue cocktail dress looked particularly pretty in the morning light. Maybe she would wear it to the homecoming dinner dance. After all, she had sewn the dress to her own measurements. Why not enjoy it?

She gathered the feather duster and her cleaning supplies and took them to the back room to get them out of the way.

When the bell on her shop door sounded, Juliette walked from the back expecting to find Tori waiting for her, but her breath caught when she saw Jude standing there with two cups of coffee in his hands.

"Good morning," he said. "I thought you could use some coffee this morning. You were still at Ethan and Chelsea's when I left last night."

He handed her the cup.

"Thanks," she said, accepting it gratefully. "Aren't you thoughtful? But you didn't say goodbye last night. When did you leave?"

"I think it was about eleven thirty. I was already outside so I walked around the house to my truck. I figured I didn't need to track anything across Chelsea's floor and I didn't want to disturb you and the girls."

"Did you and Ethan get a chance to talk?"

"We did."

"How did it go?"

Jude shrugged. "About as well as I expected."

"And that tells me absolutely nothing. Does he want first right of refusal? Is he going to buy the land?"

"I don't think so. He says it doesn't fit into his current business plan."

Jude glanced down at his cup. "Although he did bring up a good point. It isn't fair that I sprang this on him without giving him the opportunity to reevaluate his plans. He was quick to point that out last night. I need to take a step back and rethink what I'm doing. I'm not simply looking to hand off the land to someone who isn't going to respect it."

He shrugged again.

Juliette wasn't quite sure what to say, which probably meant it was a good time to change the subject.

"I thought you had a meeting in Dallas today."

Jude smiled. "I do. I just happened to see your car outside as I was driving by."

"That's the second time you've used that drive-by line on me."

"Is it?"

Juliette nodded.

"Oh, well, is it working?"

"I don't know. Why don't you drive by my place tonight after you finish with your meeting and see if you can find my car there? I can make you dinner."

She was going on pure instinct. She knew it might not be a good idea, but she hadn't been able to get peace about the way they had left things last night.

The bell on the shop door jingled again. This time Lucy and Tori stepped inside.

"Well, hello there," Tori said, making no disguise of the fact that she was looking Jude up and down and appreciating what she saw. He did look particularly good this morning. His jeans were just tight enough to accentuate his butt. His muscled shoulders and trim waist made the most of his blue plaid button-down, hinting at the sexy six-pack hidden beneath. When they'd kissed at the lake, her hands had done some exploring and he felt good. Damn him. She'd be lying if she hadn't thought about what was underneath that shirt more than once since then. Obviously, Tori noticed, too. However, Tori was simply a flirt. She knew Juliette and Jude had history and any insinuations were merely for sport.

"Good morning, ladies," Jude said. "I was just leaving. You three have a fabulous day. And I will see *you* tonight," he said to Juliette. How did he make such a simple statement sound so sexy? His gaze promised something. She wasn't sure what, but it sparked a sizzle of attraction in her veins and encouraged her lady parts to demand things that Juliette's right mind knew were not a good idea. In fact, they were downright dangerous.

She suddenly had a hunger to live on the edge.

Tori excused herself to the ladies' room to replenish her lipstick.

"What's up with you and Jude?" Lucy asked. She'd never been one to beat around the bush.

"Nothing, why?"

Lucy was eyeing her as if she were trying to read her mind. Juliette was glad she couldn't.

"Any chance of you getting back together?"

"Lucy, why the inquisition?"

Lucy held up her hands and then placed them on her baby bump. "You know there's nothing I'd love more than for you to be my sister-in-law, but you need to look out for you."

Okay, that was a jarring turn in a different direction. Ever the romantic, Lucy usually inserted herself into the role of matchmaker.

"Don't frown at me," she said. Juliette hadn't realized she'd been frowning. "What I'm trying to say is," Lucy continued, "I think there are big things in your future."

"Thank you? I think."

Her friend could be cryptic sometimes, but this was another level of puzzling even for Lucy. Maybe her pregnancy had tempered Lucy's rose-colored glasses because for once she was sounding like a realist, not a romantic. If anyone knew how discontent Juliette was, Lucy did.

"What do you mean?" Juliette asked. "What are you up to, Lucy?"

Lucy gave her the big eyes. "I'm sure I have no idea what you're talking about."

"Oh, I'm sure you do."

Lucy looked thoughtful for a moment. "Well, now that you mention it, would you ever consider selling your business to me?"

"What?" The possibility had never crossed her mind. But even at first glance, it made sense. Lucy had done wonders with the Campbell Wedding Barn. Juliette had been feeding her business left and right, especially since she had grown weary of living out of a suitcase with all the travel she'd been doing for out-of-town weddings. When Lucy had opened the doors to the wedding barn, it had given Juliette the opportunity to stay closer to home. It made sense to take local jobs and steer the business to Lucy because it cut Juliette's own expenses. The Campbell Wedding Barn had been a godsend and a win-win opportunity.

"You mentioned you're interested in making a change," Lucy said. "What if I made you an offer for your business and merged it with mine? I could be a full-service wedding operation—planning and venue. Would you be interested?"

Juliette blinked a couple of times. "I don't know. This is all so unexpected. But I'm certainly willing to consider it. Although I have no idea what I would do next if I sold the business."

Lucy snorted. "You and my brother are perfect for each other."

Juliette felt her neck turning red. "Why? What do you mean?"

"You know exactly what I mean. The two of you may have been apart for several years, but you're still perfect for each other. I hope one day you two will get it together and recognize that before the other one does something stupid like marry someone else."

Lucy's comment made the heat that had been confined to Juliette's neck blossom upward. "Luce, I have to be honest with you. I think Jude and I want very different things. Even if I do sell my business, I won't go on the road with him. I hope that's not what you're thinking. I need more than that."

Lucy flinched. "Oh, my gosh, no, that's not what I was getting at, at all. If anybody understands that, you know I do."

Lucy and Zane had been through a similar situation before they managed to make things work. Zane had landed his dream job at a top horse-breeding ranch in Ocala, Florida, when Lucy found out she was pregnant with his baby. Their main stumbling block had been that Lucy had worked hard to make the Campbell Wedding Barn the success that it was. Even so, she'd gone to Ocala with Zane to see if she could be happy there with him, maybe even start another wedding venue, but it proved not to be in the stars. In the end, it also proved not to be the be-all and end-all that Zane thought it would be. Or at least Zane ended up loving Lucy more than he loved the job and Ocala. Juliette and Jude were sort of facing a similar problem, but in reverse. Both had successful careers but were discontent and neither knew their next step. Now that Jude was home, and both of them were unencumbered by other relationships, people automatically assumed they would get back together. Even though the chemistry was still strong, they were different people than they were ten years ago. She could not plan her future around someone she used to know.

Juliette nodded. "Why don't you put together a proposal with an offer and we'll talk about it."

Lucy clapped her hands like a little girl. "Sounds good. By the way, I have something for you."

Lucy reached into her handbag, a Tori Ashford Alden design, and handed Juliette a small box. "I got you a present."

It was a box of condoms.

A hiccup of nervous laughter escaped from Juliette's throat. "Lucy! What in the world?"

Lucy threw her an incredulous look. "Do I really need to explain?"

"No," Juliette blurted, holding the small box in both hands, trying to render it invisible. As if someone might look in the window and see her holding it. Stranger things had happened.

"I just don't want you and my brother to have any *happy surprises.* Not that it's not wonderful. But you two need to sort yourselves out before you give me any little nieces and nephews. But don't wait too long, okay?"

"Lucy, it's not like that—"

"Oh, come on, Jules. I'm not your mother. You can be real with me."

"Lucy…"

Juliette started to explain that she was being real. That it had been a very long time since she and Jude had been *that* intimate. But she stopped herself. "Thanks," she said instead. "That was very thoughtful of you. I'm going to put these in my purse now."

Rather than thinking of how she and Jude would use Lucy's *gift,* she pondered what she would do if Lucy did buy her business and she was free to do anything. The possibility hit her like a blast of cool, fresh air. It took her breath away, but was refreshing and exciting in the same instant. It was the first time in her life that she might be free to do what *she* wanted to do. Granted, it had been her choice to build Weddings by Juliette. That was one way to look at it. Another way to look at it was that the business had been low-hanging fruit that had virtually fallen off the branch into her hands. It had just been too good of an opportunity to walk away from. When her mother's wedding coordinator quit out of frustration two weeks before Guinevere's marriage to Howard, Juliette picked up the ball and saved the day. Guinevere, being Guinevere, had invited every person she had ever spoken to in her life and had regaled them with the dramatic tale of how the first wedding coordinator had heartlessly left her in the lurch, but her darling daughter had not only come to her rescue, but had delivered a wedding beyond Guinevere's wildest dreams, coordinating an event the caliber of which the wayward planner could've never been capable. Of course not, Juliette mused. She had an unfair advantage since it was her mother's fifth trip down the aisle and Juliette had been her maid of honor at four of the five weddings. She knew exactly what her mother liked and how to make wedding number five bigger and better than the last three. But to Guinevere that was a minor detail not worth divulging. Every time she told the story, it got more dramatic and dire, until she'd built Juliette up to be some sort of superhuman wedding goddess. People ate it up. Inquiries began to pour in. *How much would you charge to do my wedding? My daughter is getting married and she wants a Cinderella-style wedding; could you do that? I just loved the flowers you used for Guinevere's reception. Could you re-create them for mine?*

Of course she could. She was more than happy to help and they were more than happy to pay her unheard-of fees. She had just graduated from St Andrews with a degree in management, with an eye for nonprofit work. Doing weddings had given her a temporary reprieve from having to beat the pavement to find a real job. Weddings were lucrative. Very lucrative. Sometimes she almost felt guilty charging what she did, but people were virtually throwing money at her...yet of course, she had to pacify all those bridezillas.

Ugh, the bridezillas. It might not be a bad business if not for the bridezillas.

Soon, everything snowballed and she didn't have time to think about whether or not she enjoyed planning weddings. She was too busy planning them. And the silver lining was she had a valid reason to not figure out what she wanted to do with her life, because she was too busy working.

Besides, it made Guinevere so happy. Since she had provided the springboard, her mother felt entitled to take partial credit for Juliette's success. And if it made Guinevere happy, Juliette didn't have a problem with her mother claiming a bit of the thunder.

Juliette's father—Guinevere's husband—had passed away when Juliette was just starting high school. Since that time, it seemed that Guinevere was only happy when Juliette was excelling—at something. Anything. Whether it was being crowned homecoming queen, or rodeo queen, or champion barrel racer, achieving valedictorian of her senior class, being voted most likely to succeed, or winning a scholarship to St Andrews, Juliette's accomplishments made Guinevere happy. It made Juliette happy to see her mother smile again.

But now that her mother was *mostly* happily married

to Howard, it was finally Juliette's time. It was time for her to stop putting others first—the brides, her mother, a job she didn't love—and to get a life for herself. If she sold the business, she might be able to buy herself a little time to figure out what she wanted. Maybe even take a vacation. The image of lying on a white sandy beach with azure water lapping at her feet...lying next to Jude...and how they could put that box of condoms to good use popped into her head.

No! Stop! Rewind!

Thank goodness Tori chose that moment to come back into the room. "Juliette? Who designed these dresses?" She walked straight over to the dress dummies and started inspecting the seams. "These are cute and very well made."

"I sewed them, but they're not my designs. Zane's mother, Dorothy, was a fabulous seamstress and used to sketch fashion designs in a little notebook she kept. A couple of months ago, the town had a memorial. Lucy and I both sew and we brought some of Dorothy's designs to life for it."

"She's being modest," Lucy said. "Dorothy's sketches were pretty basic. Juliette came up with all of the finishes. Actually, didn't you basically redesign the blue cocktail dress?"

"Well, I changed it up quite a bit, but these are Dorothy's designs. I can't take credit for them."

"They are quite good. You had mentioned that you were in a place where you might want a change. Have you ever considered working for a fashion house? More specifically my fashion house?"

Chapter Seven

"I wish I had better news for you, Jude," said Clive Curtis, the vice president of sales and marketing for Copenhagen Sporting Goods. "The bottom line is sales for the On-Off line have fallen off dramatically since you haven't been able to compete. That's why we decided to postpone the photo shoot. Thanks for understanding. I still wanted you to come in today so that we could meet face-to-face. You know, mano a mano. Because I want you to know even though others may be questioning Copenhagen's relationship with Jude Campbell, I'm still on your side. I'm your advocate."

Curtis paused and slurped his coffee.

"I'm not going to lie—it was a hard sell convincing the powers that be to renew your sponsorship since you're not riding in the championship this year. I got them to entertain it on the contingency that you compete next year. I can guarantee you if you opt out next season, not only will you lose the sponsorship, but we will be forced to eighty-six the On-Off line. Like I said, I'm sorry. I hate to be the bearer of bad news. But it's in your hands. If you look at it in a positive light you're the one who has all the power here. You can say yes and voilà, you've got Copenhagen at your feet. You say no…" Curtis shrugged. "Like I said, I'm really sorry."

He didn't look sorry. And even less so when his attention flicked to a message that flashed on his smartphone. And what a load of bull that Copenhagen would ever be at his feet. They already had one foot out the door. Did Curtis think he was stupid?

"We're going to need a commitment from you by the end of next week." He said the words robotically as he replied to the text. "So unless you have any more questions… I think we're done here."

Jude glanced at his agent, waiting for Bob to jump in and do the negotiation thing he paid him to do, but the guy just sat there mute, drumming his fingers on the table.

"So let me get this straight," Jude said. "You're dropping my line if I don't ride next year."

Curtis didn't even glance up from his phone. "Yeah. And the sponsorship, too. I guess that's the long and short of it."

The words hung between them. Bob was still mute.

"Okay," Curtis said, setting down his phone. "To show you I'm not totally unreasonable, I think I can convince them to push off your giving us an answer until we meet at the Bull Rider Expo in Vegas, the week of the twenty-third. Maybe you'll be feeling better by then. You know, more like yourself. I don't want you to think we're being hard to work with. I know you've got to look out for number one. You've got to take care of your health. We get it. We do. It's all good. And if you're not up for riding at the expo, we can put you at a table and have you sign autographs. Maybe sign some shirts."

Autographs? Jude swallowed a wave of rage. The guy was acting like Jude was sitting out to nurse a cold. Not because he'd suffered three concussions over a span of three months. This would've been a good time for Bob to chime in, but he didn't.

That was another relationship that needed reevaluating.

Jude understood that business was business. The bottom line was the bottom line. He had never expected anyone to hand him anything. It was a given that the sponsorship would go away if he didn't ride next year, but he had been hoping that the On-Off line might be strong enough that they would want to continue it—hell, he'd even be willing to promote it to increase sales since its success would buy him some time.

It looked like he was going to have to come up with a plan faster than he'd realized.

Curtis stood and held out his hand. "Always a pleasure." Jude shook it.

"Thanks for coming out here to meet with us. As I said, these things are always better handled mano a mano."

Mano a mano. Was that his catchphrase?

Jude wondered if Curtis understood that *mano a mano* didn't mean "man-to-man." It meant "hand-to-hand," as in hand-to-hand combat. But at this point, Jude wasn't going to correct him.

Franklin barked at the knock on Juliette's front door.

"Who is it, Franklin?" she asked as she dried her hands on the dishcloth. She was making chicken piccata for dinner. It was one of her go-to dishes. She loved to cook, but one of the hazards of being a workaholic and living alone was that she did not indulge in the activity enough. Inviting Jude over tonight had been a good excuse to play in the kitchen... And spend time with him.

She checked her reflection in the mirror over the console table in the foyer before opening the door.

"Franklin, sit. You're a good boy, but you need to use your manners."

The dog lowered his haunches to the floor and stared up at her for approval.

"Good boy," she said as she opened the door.

"I'm glad somebody thinks so," Jude said. He was carrying two bottles of wine—the white wine would go perfectly with the chicken piccata—and a six-pack of beer. "Oh, were you talking to the dog?"

At the sound of the word *dog*, Franklin broke rank and jumped up, putting his front paws on Jude's jean-clad legs. He squatted down, setting the beer and wine on either side of him and petted the dog, who proceeded to kiss him hello.

"Not on the lips, please," Jude said. "The lips are reserved for someone special."

"Oh yeah?" said Juliette. "Do I know her?"

Jude stood, smiled. "I think you do."

For a moment, Juliette thought he might kiss her. She would've wagered that he was thinking about it, maybe weighing it against the no-strings, no-pressure agreement they'd made last night. She contemplated leaning in and taking the initiative—

"I wasn't sure what would go best with dinner, so I brought both red and white. And whatever it is, it smells delicious."

"Good. Are you hungry?" She led the way into the kitchen. He followed.

"Starving."

"Help yourself to some cheese and fix yourself a drink. Dinner will be ready in about twenty minutes. How did your day go?"

"Not at all as I had planned." He opened the stainless-steel refrigerator door. "Is it okay if I stash these in here to keep them cold?" He gestured to the beer. He had set the bottles of wine on the counter.

"Knock yourself out."

Juliette had remodeled her kitchen a year and a half ago, complete with an Electrolux refrigerator and a Viking professional-grade gas range. It was a lot of kitchen for someone who didn't have much of a chance to cook, but even looking at it made her happy. It was her touchstone, a reminder that it would be waiting for her when she was ready.

The upside to not doing much cooking was that she had plenty of room in the refrigerator. She had stopped by the grocery store on her way home from work to pick up the provisions that she needed for dinner: boneless skinless chicken breasts, eggs, bread crumbs, butter and lemons. She had used the last of an open bottle of white wine; she had capers in the refrigerator and parsley in her herb garden. She would pair the chicken with mashed potatoes and sautéed green beans. Voilà—a delicious meal in no time.

"Wine or beer?" he asked.

"Wine, please." She took down a pilsner glass and two wine goblets from the cabinet next to the refrigerator in case he wanted to switch to wine with dinner. She handed him the pilsner and set one wineglass next to the bottle. She had already set the table, so she placed the extra wineglass at the place she had set for Jude.

"Tell me about the meeting," she said.

He grimaced as he opened the bottle of wine with the waiter's corkscrew Juliette had fished out of the utensil drawer. Pretty deft for a cowboy, she thought as she watched him coax the cork out of the bottle.

"In a minute. First, tell me something good. Anything that's good."

Uh-oh. That didn't bode well for his day.

"Something good? Let me see… Remember Tabatha, the bride you saw the other day at the wedding barn?"

"The one with purple shoes and road rage?"

"Yes, that's the one," she laughed. "I had a friend of mine re-dye the shoes and Tabatha couldn't have been happier. She actually hugged me when she saw them."

"And you say your job isn't fulfilling."

"It does have its moments. Oh, but something else

interesting came up today. Lucy talked to me about possibly buying Weddings by Juliette."

Jude's eyebrows shot up.

"Yes, she wants to merge it with the Campbell Wedding Barn, which is actually a really good idea. She is going to get a proposal together and we're going to meet within the week to see what we can come up with."

"You're really serious about getting out of the business then?"

"Serious as a final markdown sale at Bloomingdale's."

"That sounds very serious. But I'll have to take your word for it. Well, good, if you are unemployed, you'll have to come on the road with me."

"Here we go again," Juliette said, keeping her voice light. "Does that mean you made a decision today?"

Jude shook his head. "It was a weird day. It's a good thing you didn't come with me. They postponed the photo shoot until after I commit to another year on the circuit."

"Yikes," Juliette said. "Does that mean the clothing line is contingent on your riding, too?"

"It looks like that's the way it's shaking down. My agent is pressuring me to go one more season. The guy barely said a word in the meeting, but he had big opinions as soon as we left."

"It sounds like he doesn't have your best interest at heart, Jude," she said as she turned the chicken breasts. "Surely, he knows about the dangers of multiple concussions?"

Jude shrugged again. "He thinks he does. He says

champions don't get hurt. That's why they get the big bucks."

"I know it's been a long time," she said. "But I hope I still know you well enough to believe you are going to do the right thing—the healthy thing."

Jude shrugged.

"I don't know. It's a lot to consider. I would be giving up a lot to retire early. You know, financial plans included me riding at least one more year."

"Yeah, but if you get hurt again, it might be even more costly."

She could read his energy, feel him bristle, virtually see the walls go up. To lighten the mood, she changed tactics.

"If you could do anything in the world, if money didn't matter, what would you do?" she asked. "I've been thinking a lot about that myself. I mean, if Lucy buys my business, it'll be a nice nest egg. It won't be enough for me to retire at twenty-eight, but it will be capital for something else."

She took plates from the table and started dishing up the meal.

"I just realized," Jude said, "I don't even know what you studied at that fancy college you went to. I remember when we were in high school, you always wanted to work with kids."

His smile put her at ease. He was more like himself again.

"You have a good memory. I studied management, with an emphasis in nonprofit. I always thought I would work for some sort of children's charity after graduation. Or maybe something for displaced women and children. And here I am, the bridezilla's handmaiden. Isn't it funny the places that life leads you?"

She set the plates on the table as he refilled her wineglass and poured some for himself.

"I always admired that about you. Your soft spot for kids—not the bridezilla's handmaiden bit."

They laughed and clinked wineglasses.

"In fact, I think a little bit of your good influence must've rubbed off on me. The thing that rankles me the most about losing the On-Off line if I don't go another season is that the kids' charity won't get the proceeds from the sales of my line anymore. In the grand scheme of things, what I contribute is probably like a bucket of water out of the ocean, but it's something."

He shrugged and took a bite of the chicken. "This is delicious. When did you become a good cook?"

"You know, just because Copenhagen pulls out of the deal, that doesn't mean you couldn't start your own thing."

"My own 'thing'? That sounds official."

"You know what I mean."

"Actually, I've had this thought of starting a bull riding school. A place where all kids who are interested can learn and no one is turned away because they can't afford it. My dad was never supportive—financially or emotionally. You know how he was. He could be such a tight-ass. He'd made up his mind that since he hadn't been able to make bull riding work, he didn't want me to outshine him. Remember how I had to sneak around to get any kind of experience at all? He sure as hell wasn't going to pay for lessons. You would've thought I was dealing drugs or something the way I had to hide it from him. But he was hell-bent on keeping me from it."

Jude had a far-off look in his eye.

"Maybe he was concerned about your safety?" Juliette offered. "It's a pretty rough sport."

Juliette knew that wasn't altogether true. Donovan Campbell had been a hard-edged, hard-to-know man who seemed to love the bottle more than he loved his own son. She had witnessed Mr. Campbell and Jude coming to verbal blows more often than she wanted to remember. The two clashed, but until that last night—the night that changed everything—he hadn't been physically abusive. But that night Donovan Campbell had nearly beaten Jude to a bloody pulp.

When Juliette got word of what had happened, she'd found Jude at the cabin. It was the first place she'd looked. She'd known instinctively that she would find him there. It was the night before she was supposed to leave for St Andrews. Emotions had been running high. Jude had been working for his father, keeping the books for the Triple C Ranch, because Donovan had been determined to find a place in the family business for his spirited son. The family business had come natural to Ethan, but Jude had often told her that the thought of spending his life at the Triple C had made him feel as fenced in as the horses they bred.

On the afternoon of Juliette's last night in Celebration, Don had discovered that Jude had made a mistake in the ledger. His dyslexia had caused him to transpose two numbers, recording an entry that should have been

$1,925 as $9,125. By inadvertently transposing those two numbers, checks had bounced and it had cost Mr. Campbell a lot of money to fix the error. He took the cost out on Jude's hide.

When Juliette found Jude at the cabin, he was a bloody mess. She'd nursed his wounds, cleaning them and bandaging them up and holding him until he was himself again.

Or so she'd thought.

One minute Jude had been sobbing on her shoulder and the next minute he was proposing marriage. He wanted to elope.

Let's go, he'd said. *Let's get out of town and leave all of this behind. We'll get married and we'll make a life for ourselves somewhere else. Juliette, I love you. Please say you'll be my wife.*

She'd loved him. Of course she'd loved him, but running away with him would've meant giving up St Andrews, giving up her scholarship—giving up the life that Guinevere had so painstakingly orchestrated for her. If she ran away what would become of her mother, who was already heartbroken over losing her husband?

Juliette hadn't meant for him to take her refusal as a final, terminating *no*. She'd tried to make him understand she was just saying *not right now*, but Jude had freaked. They'd fought. He'd left the cabin. She'd left for Scotland the next day. They hadn't even said goodbye.

They hadn't talked much her first semester abroad. Only once or twice. International calls were expensive. He'd left home to go on the road, entering every competition for which he could scrounge up money. But while she was away at college that first term, the most important thing she'd learned was that she didn't want to live without him.

The next time she saw him, three months later, it was Christmas. Her gift to him was going to be that she was giving up St Andrews so that they could start their life together. It was supposed to be a surprise.

She'd been willing to give up everything to be with him, but he'd come home engaged to someone else. Juliette had left before Jude even knew she was at home.

Juliette blinked away the thought. He hadn't married the girl he'd brought home. He'd admitted she'd been a rebound. That she hadn't been *her*. But still—

She suddenly realized no matter how hurt she'd been or how she'd tried to shut Jude out, she'd never stopped loving him.

"My dad would get such satisfaction if he could see me now," Jude said.

"Well, yeah, you're the reigning world champion."

"I am the lame duck world champion, one concussion away from permanent brain damage and I don't even get to defend my title this year. I can almost hear him calling me a loser from beyond the grave."

"Is that what this is all about?" Juliette reached across the table and put her hand on Jude's. "You know there's no shame in retiring now. Jude, you don't have anything to prove to anyone. If anything, I would think that you should be pretty darn proud of yourself."

Jude turned his hand over so that they were palm to palm. He ran his thumb along the side of her hand. The feeling of his skin on hers—even if it was just their hands touching—sent tingles of longing sparking through her. There was something so sensual about it, that him touching her so innocently was so sexy.

"My dad died three months later. The last thing he said to me was, 'You're a disappointment. You're never going to amount to anything.' I guess that's why I can't be happy until I prove him wrong."

"Jude—"

Franklin started barking at the sound of the front door opening. It startled them out of their reverie.

"*Hel-luuu!* Juliette?" Guinevere's voice rang out. "Are you at home?"

The sound of something rolling on the hardwood floor preceded Guinevere's appearance in the kitchen.

"There you are." Gripping the handle of an oversize suitcase, Guinevere stiffened and raised her chin, literally looking down her nose at Jude. "Oh. I didn't realize you had company." Her voice was flat.

Jude stood. Juliette knew it was out of respect for her mother, but something about the scene took her back to high school and the days of Guinevere walking in at inopportune moments. Her mother had never cared for Jude and catching them together in what might suggest a compromising situation always made matters tense. Even though this "compromising situation" was only an innocent dinner.

"Mother, Jude's truck is in the driveway," Juliette said. "How could you miss it?"

"Yes, I suppose it is." She sighed. "Hello, Jude. I heard you were back in town."

"Mother," Juliette admonished, embarrassed by the derisive tone of her mother's voice.

Guinevere's expression suggested she smelled something foul. Some things never changed.

"Hello, Mrs. Albright. It's nice to see you."

Guinevere sniffed. "Did I interrupt your dinner?"

"We were just finishing," Juliette said. "What's with the suitcase? Are you going somewhere?"

"I'm leaving Howard."

"What?" Juliette asked. Jude seemed to freeze in place.

"You heard me. I've had it. I am leaving that man."

Juliette hadn't been home to talk her mother off the ledge with husbands two, three and four. Or to hold her hand through the legitimate hard times. But Howard seemed so different. He seemed good for her. Her mother and Howard never had any of the red flags that Juliette used to identify in some of her clients—that she had seen with Guinevere and her middle three marriages that happened between her father and Howard. Those red flags suggested that the marriage might have a difficult time. While Guinevere wasn't a piece of cake to live with, she and Howard seemed to balance each other—they seemed good for each other and they seemed to adore each other.

Whatever had happened was all probably a big misunderstanding, but she wasn't going to ask for details in front of Jude. She would let her mother stay here tonight, let her cool off and then help her figure things out tomorrow.

Even though Guinevere could be a handful, one of

the best pieces of advice her mother had ever given her was to not make big decisions when you were hungry, tired or overheated.

"I'll go," said Jude. "It sounds like you two have a lot to talk about. Thanks for dinner."

"No, don't go," Juliette said.

Guinevere tutted. "Juliette, dear, if Jude says he needs to go, let him go."

"Mom, he wasn't going to leave until you appeared."

When Juliette was in high school, her mother had staunchly maintained that Juliette was too young to get serious about a boy. She needed to see the world—meet a prince. Guinevere had insisted that Juliette was destined to marry a prince and she didn't mean that figuratively. She meant an actual prince, as in the William and Harry variety. She claimed to have sent Juliette's photo to Prince Harry, though her mother never would say exactly where she'd sent it. She let her mother have her fantasy. It'd kept her off the scent of Juliette falling head over heels for Jude. He may not have been a prince by Guinevere's standards, but he'd ruled the kingdom of Juliette's heart.

Juliette pushed to her feet. "Mom, why don't you go ahead and unpack? I made some extra chicken and potatoes. Help yourself to it. Take a bath and relax. Jude and I are going out for a while. I will be back later."

"Where are you going?" Guinevere put her hands on her hips.

Juliette mirrored her stance. "Mom, you're at my house. You don't get to ask the questions. I'll see you later."

She motioned with her head for Jude to follow and grabbed her purse and sweater off the console table in the foyer before they stepped out into the chilly October night.

When the two stepped outside, Jude said, "Hey, if you need to stay—"

"Absolutely not. I think she could use some time by herself. Let's go to your cabin."

"Okay, I'm certainly not going to challenge that," Jude said, smiling as he opened his truck door for her and helped her inside.

Chapter Eight

Jude entered the dark cabin first. He flicked on the light and held the door so that Juliette could enter.

The place was a small, functional studio with a living area that doubled as a bedroom. It also had a kitchenette and bathroom. He hadn't counted on having company tonight. Everything lay exactly as he'd left it when he left this morning. The morning paper was askew on the wooden table, next to a scattering of coins he'd taken out of his pocket and a coffee cup he'd intended to wash when he got home. A small couch and coffee table sat along one wall and a bed pushed into the opposite corner took up most of the living space. He'd made the bed when he'd gotten up.

Making his bed was a habit. While he was on the road, he lived in a trailer that he pulled along behind his truck because it was more economical than staying in hotels. He didn't have the advantage of maid service. So he had gotten used to making his own bed.

He'd sold the trailer the day before he'd come home. The small cash infusion would allow him to pay his property tax and keep the land afloat until he figured out what he was going to do next.

Juliette turned in a tight circle, looking at everything. "Wow. I haven't been in here since—"

She clamped her mouth shut as if she suddenly remembered the last time they were there.

He remembered.

The sweet and salty memory of the last time they'd been here together made his heart race and his blood course. The fact that they were here together again made every cell in his body dance.

"It's been a long time," she finally said. She was still wearing the sweater she'd grabbed on the way out of her house and clutching the handle of her purse like it was a lifeline.

He nodded. Maybe it wasn't a good idea that they'd come here. But it was too late now.

The events that had transpired that long-ago night hung between them like a ghost they couldn't exorcise until they talked about it.

"Do you want to take off your sweater?" he offered. "You can put your purse down, too. I promise I won't steal it. It's a safe neighborhood."

He had a habit of using humor to lighten a tense mood. Some people accused him of never taking anything seriously, but he never meant any harm.

"I know this neighborhood well," she said.

"I know you do. But you don't come around here much anymore, do you?"

"Neither do you."

He shrugged and nodded at the same time.

"I think we need to finish talking about what we were discussing before my mother interrupted."

She set her purse on the table and slid out of her sweater.

"Let's sit down." He motioned to the couch, and then walked to the fridge, where he grabbed two beers and popped the tops. "I didn't know we would be here tonight or I would've gotten you some wine."

"Beer is fine," she said as she took one of the bottles that he offered. Their hands touched in the process.

"We don't have to stay here if it makes you uncomfortable," he said as he sat down beside her. "We could go somewhere else."

"No. This is fine. I like it here. In fact, I was disappointed that I didn't get to come inside the other day we came out here. But you're changing the subject again. You have a bad habit of doing that, and you should know I'm on to you."

She smiled, but he could see something that looked like uncertainty in her eyes.

"Are you okay?" Juliette asked. "Talk to me, Jude. What you said about your father…is that why you're considering another season?"

"Yeah. It is. Maybe. Partially. But I don't want to talk about it right now. There's nothing more to say and my dad has already ruined too many things for me. I'm not going to let him have tonight, too."

She opened her mouth like she was going to say something, but then closed it again. When she finally did speak, she said, "How is it that we went all these years without talking, Jude?"

"You have no idea how many times I've asked myself that same question," he said.

"Why didn't you…try?" she said.

"I could ask you the same thing."

The air stilled. The haints of the past crowded between them.

"When the man who had asked you to give up everything and elope with him—to spend the rest of your life with him—shows up three months later engaged to someone else, it makes it a little hard to be the first one to reach out."

He nodded. "Fair enough. That's why I came to see you first thing when I got into town."

"This was probably a bad idea." She started to push to a standing position but, with a strong arm, Jude pulled her down next to him. "No, it's not."

And he kissed her.

Damn if she didn't kiss him back. Drinking in the life breath of him as if making up for lost time. This kiss was different than the one they'd shared right outside the cabin on his first day back. That one was tender and tentative. It spoke of promise, yet offered room for retreat. And she had retreated. Or at least she'd tried.

This kiss was possessive—it threatened to swallow her up. It demanded to know: *What next?*

When they came up for air, Jude looked wild-eyed. "I never wanted to hurt you, Jules. I wanted to marry you."

She held her breath, wondering if he was going to add the three words she both longed and dreaded to hear: *I still do.*

But the moment passed. And it was a good thing because it gave her a moment to compose herself.

Was that why he'd come home? Was it why he'd come straight to her?

"Why didn't you marry— What was her name? I mean, it doesn't matter."

But it does.

It still mattered, even though she wished it didn't. Ten years was a long time ago, but in some regards, it felt like yesterday.

"Her name was Glori. She wasn't you."

"What?"

"I couldn't marry her because she wasn't you."

His words knocked the breath out of her. She put some space between them by leaning her head back on the couch cushions and staring up at the ceiling.

She wasn't you.

Juliette hated herself for getting so much satisfaction out of that. She wasn't happy that someone else may have been hurt. But Jude was *hers*. He always had been. Always would…

"Is that why you never married anyone else?" she pressed.

"I don't see a ring on your finger," he quipped, but

quickly softened his tone. "I'm sure it wasn't for lack of opportunities. When you were busy owning Europe, I'm sure any number of Euro princes would've abdicated their thrones to have you."

"If you think flattery is going to get you anywhere—"

He leaned down and kissed her again, long and slow.

"Why? Will it?" he said into her lips before taking possession of her mouth.

His hand slipped from the back of her head and migrated to her breast. He touched her tentatively at first, as if waiting for her to stop him. But she didn't want him to stop.

She craved him.

His fingertips meandered down her belly to the hem of her dress and found their way underneath. He traced tiny circles on her belly, brushing away what was left of her better judgment. Most of it had taken the night off, leaving her to fend for herself when it came to saving herself from the inevitable heartbreak of Jude Campbell.

But she was way past the point of no return, and right now, right here with Jude was the only place she wanted to be.

A growl came from deep inside Jude's throat as he lost himself in her, in them. The feel of her body in his arms unleashed a greedy beast in him that did not want to wait. It needed her *now*. He needed her now.

Without breaking the kiss, he pulled her to her feet, intending to walk her backward toward the bed, but somehow they ended up pressed against the wall next to the bed. She slid her arms around his neck. He ran his hands down her sides, wedging them between her smooth body and the rough wooden paneling on the wall. He slid them down until he'd taken possession of her perfectly round butt. He cupped her rear, pulling her even closer, exploring her neck with his mouth. She smelled so good, like flowers and fresh sunshine. He lingered for a moment, savoring the scent of her and the feel of their bodies pressed against each other.

She met him halfway.

She felt so good. But he needed more. He ran one of his hands down the back of her thigh until he found the bend in her knee and brought her leg to his hip so that they fit together. Puzzle pieces. Lock and key.

Every inch of him needed her. Even if he hadn't been conscious of it before, he'd wanted to hold her like this, feel her just like this, from the moment he saw her standing there talking to herself in the middle of Lucy's barn. The desire had grown as they'd sat in the Redbird and reminisced and laughed like old friends and now it was so great it had rendered him half out of his mind.

Even so, he hadn't planned on seducing her—or had she seduced him? That was the thing about them. They tended to spontaneously combust when they were around each other. Sometimes it was difficult to discern where one of them stopped and the other began.

How *had* they gone so long without each other?

It became clear that he had been waiting for the right time to come back to her.

He'd wanted to come back a success. He'd wanted everyone to believe he was worthy of her. He'd waited because it had taken too long to convince himself that he was. No matter what he did, his dad would never believe he was worthy...of anything.

He'd had the brass ring in his hands and then he'd lost it—

No! Stop thinking.

He wasn't going to ruin this. He wasn't going to let Donovan Campbell ruin this.

He pressed his pelvis against her. And she answered by pushing back.

"God, Juliette..." he whispered against her mouth.

She fisted her hands into the collar of his shirt and held on to him, smothering his words with her lips and kissing him deeply, frantically.

He pulled his head back just slightly to look down at them. Her dress was pushed up around her waist. His shirt was askew. He ran his palms up her curves until he got to her dress. Impatiently, he tugged it up and over her head. She helped him by wiggling out of it.

Reverently, he ran his fingertips over the lace-covered bra, before delving beneath the frilly surface. He savored the feel of her skin. Even after all these years, she was so familiar. She felt like coming home. Like the home he'd needed all his life. His lips found her neck. His tongue teased a trail to the tender spot at the base of her ear. He nuzzled her temple, kissed her eyes, her right cheekbone, her chin, finally reclaiming her lips. He was breathless and crazy drunk on the taste of her, the feel of her.

She answered him by yanking his shirttails out of his pants. She undid the first two buttons, but grew impatient and didn't bother undoing the rest. She just pulled the shirt up and over his head, letting it fall to the floor.

His fingers worked the hooks of her bra—light blue lace, with matching panties. Pushing it aside, he lowered his head and found her nipple, taking it into his mouth. She cried out. It was the most beautiful song he'd ever heard.

She moved her hands to his waist and then around to his butt, pulling him against her. She made another noise, this one deep in her throat.

He helped her out of her bra, almost hating to remove the delicate lace. It was sexy, erotic, but what waited underneath had even more promise. As her bra fell to the floor, he slid a hand down her hips, hooking his thumbs in the elastic ribbons that were connected to the scant triangle that barely covered her center. He tugged them lower and lower until they fell away.

He slid his hand between her legs. God, she was just as turned on as he was.

Slow the hell down, man. Slow way down.

One way to reset the pace was to move over to the bed. But she was having no part of that until she had gotten rid of the last barrier between them. She undid the button on his jeans, lowered his zipper and tugged away the offending fabric. As she took him in her hands, he was afraid he was going to come undone at the feel of her touch.

"Do you have a condom?" she murmured.

"Somewhere," he said, a little dazed.

"Wait, actually, I have one." She put some space between them. It was a sobering move.

"You have one?"

"Yeah. Just a sec. It's in my purse. Hold on."

He hated to let go of her. He should have been better prepared, but this was the last place he thought they'd end up tonight. But things had changed. In a drastic way. And he certainly wasn't complaining.

"Don't go away." She kissed him. "I'll be right back."

His groin grew even tighter as he watched her walk across the room to the table.

"Did you plan on seducing me tonight?" He laughed. "Because if you did that is fine with me. Just hurry up."

"No, I didn't. This was a gift." She held up the silver packet. "It's compliments of some very good friends who obviously know me better than I know myself."

She turned off the lights. The only thing illuminating the room was the full moon streaming in through the slats of the blinds. She made her way back to him and pushed him down onto the bed.

"Allow me," she said, getting onto her knees. She made haste in unwrapping the condom and tossing away the foil, but after that, she slowed down. She took her time with him, stroking him, kissing him until he got so close to the edge he didn't know if he could handle it anymore.

"Juliette," he pleaded. "Please. If you keep that up, I don't know how much longer I can last."

She sheathed him and then straddled him.

She was so beautiful.

He was desperate for her, but he wanted this moment to last. He had no choice but to purposely slow things down. He slid his hand between her thighs and explored her with his fingers. She was more than ready for him and just the feel of her—so wet—caused a moan to escape from deep in his throat.

"I need you inside me," she said. "Now."

He turned her over onto her back and situated himself between her thighs. She helped him find his way inside her. As he buried himself in her, it felt as if their souls had become one. Another deep groan escaped from his throat. If he'd been half out of his mind earlier, he'd completely lost it now. He was way past thinking sensibly.

But by the grace of something sacred, he managed to hold still long enough to get control of himself. Then, when he was in charge again, he began to move, and she matched him move for move until they rediscovered that timeless rhythm that was their very own. They'd always been so good together. They still were.

She slid her arms around his neck, holding on tight as he plunged deeper and deeper. Every thrust brought them closer together, closer to the edge of delight that was on the not-so-distant horizon, where they could spill over into breathless, crazy-good ecstasy.

As the rhythm got more and more intense, Juliette tightened around him—her muscles clenched and released. As she cried out, they went over the edge together.

When he finally came back down to earth, Jude was completely out of breath; his whole body was spent. She was panting and holding on to him as if he was her life preserver. They lay like that, holding each other for a very long time, until their breathing returned to normal and the world started turning again.

"I want to hold you forever," Jude said. "Do you think you could live happily in my arms, here in this cabin with me?"

"If you keep doing to me what you just did, I know I could be happy right here," she said, snuggling closer to him. She meant it. This was the closest to heaven she'd been in ages. Maybe since the last time they'd been together.

But what now? As right as it felt, maybe jumping into...*things* with him hadn't been a very smart idea. Had she just set herself up for the biggest hurt of her life—losing him again?

Even so, Juliette nuzzled into the crook of his shoulder. She couldn't help herself.

He held her tighter. His other arm was thrown across his eyes, and she could still tell that his eyes were closed.

"I've never done this before," she whispered.

"What?" he said. His voice sounded drowsy. "Yes, you have. I know that for a fact."

Juliette gave his shoulder a little push. "No, I'm talking about no-strings-attached sex."

"Is that what you want?"

He pulled away and propped himself up on his elbow. She gazed up at him, glad she could see his face.

Juliette prided herself on being decisive, on knowing her own mind and being in charge of her emotions. Yet here she was—a tangled-up mess.

A naked, tangled-up mess. Lying here with a man who had broken her heart and crushed her spirit and she needed to talk about it.

"No, it's not what I want. Not exactly. That's why I've never made a practice of having casual sex. It's always been within the boundaries of commitment. This sort of free-floating thing between us is weird for me. It will just take some getting used to."

"Are you writing us off just like that?" Jude asked.

"No, I guess I'm just preparing myself. I'm afraid of getting hurt again. I loved you, Jude. For a long time, I thought I never wanted to be in love again."

"I love you, Jules. I still love you." He kissed her temple and ran his rope-roughened hand over her sensitive skin. It felt glorious.

"Then promise me you will stay. It could be so easy if you would just stay. Retire from the circuit. Make a life here with me."

She pulled the covers up a little more and crossed her arms in front of her, feeling exposed.

Jude's arm closed around her and pulled her in closer as he lowered himself next to her.

Their bodies were close, but he wasn't saying anything. It made her mind go in a million different directions. She took everything so seriously these days. Even the feel of the pad of his thumb grazing her nipple didn't distract. It only reminded her of her nakedness—and how vulnerable she felt.

His thumb stilled. She could've sworn his breathing did, too.

"I want to promise you a lot of things," he said. "But

I don't know if I can promise you that. I need to get myself into a position where I can take care of you. And I can't promise you I'm not going to ride one more year."

"But, Jude, I have enough money that I can take care of both of us."

"There's a dozen reasons pushing me toward it and at the top of that list is that I don't want to take advantage of you."

He withdrew his arms and crossed them over his bare chest.

"I have some major responsibilities. I can't come into this unless we're equal, because that really would make me a loser who never amounted to anything except living off his girlfriend."

Juliette turned over onto her stomach so that she could see Jude's eyes.

"It would be a partnership," she offered. "I'd get us started and you would contribute. I know you would. There are lots of ways to contribute to a new enterprise without a cash investment. I mean, say I wanted to start a bull riding school. I might bring the capital, but I would have no clue about the inner workings of the operation."

"The best way to learn is to come on the road with me. Watch and learn." He smiled that smile and raked his fingers through the hair at her temple. She knew he was trying to distract her.

"I'm not going to do that, Jude."

"Okay, it looks like we're at a crossroads. Either we can get upset or we can salvage the night. Frankly, I vote for salvaging the night."

He slipped his hand between her legs and began teasing her to go again. And, damn him, damn her body, she was responding. She still loved him. They still had time for her to convince him to stay—but not right now.

His fingers were working their magic and her touch had him ready to go again. But his cell phone rang, sounding from somewhere in the heap of clothes on the floor.

It rang four times, then stopped. The interruption didn't deter him; he leaned in and kissed her, pulling her on top of him.

His phone sounded. Again.

Juliette pulled back. "Should you answer that?"

"Answer what?"

By that time the phone was silent again.

"If someone's calling this late, Jude, it might be important," she said. "If you want to get it, I won't go anywhere."

You should use the opportunity to get dressed and tell him you need to go. You should go. Now.

"Nothing is as important as this."

His deft fingers coaxed a moan out of her and all thoughts but the feel of his hands on her body and the hard length of him in her hand evaporated.

Until the damn phone rang *again*.

"Jude, please answer that." She got out of bed and fished his phone out of the pocket of his jeans.

"Here." She handed it to him. "Just answer it."

So they'll stop calling.

She'd stolen a peek at the name displayed on the LCD screen. "It's someone named Bob."

"Yeah, that's my agent. I assigned him a special ring tone. That's why I wasn't in any hurry to answer it."

"So talk to him. See what he wants. Tell him you're busy."

Juliette picked up her dress off the floor and covered herself with it as she sat down on the side of the bed.

"It's not that easy," Jude murmured as he tossed the phone toward the foot of the bed.

He didn't have to say another word for her to know Bob was probably calling him to pressure him about the season. Jude probably didn't want to talk in front of her because he'd already made up his mind.

Her heart squeezed. Suddenly, she felt exposed and vulnerable. Her eyes stung with unshed tears, which was crazy. He hadn't promised her anything. She'd even been talking about sex with no commitment. Where were these expectations coming from? Feeling his eyes on her, she slipped her dress over her head—as much to hide the threatening tears as to cover herself.

"I need to go home. Obviously, you have some things you need to take care of that you can't do while I'm here."

He reached out and touched her arm. "I wish you'd stay."

She stood up and retrieved her panties. Slid into them.

Ugh. Jude had driven her out here. Unless she wanted to walk home, she was at his mercy.

She wasn't good at things like this. Then again, she didn't know what *this* was—other than a big mistake.

"Jules?"

She didn't answer.

"Jules, look at me, please."

When she glanced up, he was sitting on the side of the bed, the old comforter draped loosely over his lap. She dug her nails into her palms to keep herself from giving in to the tears that threatened.

"The only thing I want to take care of is what we were doing before we were interrupted."

His eyes crinkled at the corners and danced with that same old Jude mirth that had always drawn people to him. He was charming that way. It wasn't that everything was a joke. He just had a lighthearted, breezy way about him that made people like him. That made women forget what was good for them and drop their panties in the middle of the floor. She felt her neck turning red and wished that she had some place to hide until it subsided, but she didn't. Even though she was fully clothed now, she felt exposed and 100 percent vulnerable to him.

"Jude, it's not that I'm trying to keep you from achieving your dream. You have to understand I would never do that. It's just that this is so dangerous. I don't think I could bear it if I lost you."

He stood up and slung the blanket around his middle. It rode dangerously low on his hips. The image of him standing there in all his sexy glory let her eyes confirm everything the feel of him had promised as they'd made love—the broad shoulders, the muscled chest, the washboard abs. Juliette's mouth went dry. No wonder he'd caused such a sensation when that bull had torn off his shirt and he'd appeared bare-chested on national TV.

He was beautiful.

The people at Copenhagen would be idiots to let him go. She would be an idiot to let him go.

"I think that means you still love me."

Yes.

No!

Liar.

"I'm still in love with you. I never stopped loving you and if you feel the same way, we will find a way to make this work."

Not if he couldn't let go of this obsession to be on top.

"I don't know. I need to go. Will you take me home? My mom's there and—" She shook her head. "I know I'm not a teenager anymore, but I need some time to think about things."

The more she was around him, the harder it was going to be to say goodbye when he left. Because from the sounds of things, it seemed like he had already made up his mind to leave.

Chapter Nine

"Whose car is that?" Jude asked when he pulled up in front of Juliette's house.

"It's Howard's," Juliette said. "I'm glad he's here. Maybe he can talk some sense into my mother."

Jude had to park behind Howard's Lincoln, which was parked next to Guinevere's car in the driveway. Juliette's Prius was in the garage, where she always parked it. If everyone kept converging at her house, maybe she should start parking in the driveway so she wouldn't be blocked in. But that was the least of her worries right now.

She sat in Jude's truck for a moment, gazing at the front porch. The light was on. It glowed a soft amber. Her mother must've turned it on, maybe when Howard arrived. He was a good man. Proof of that was that he was here, no doubt trying to win her mother back. Guinevere wasn't an easy person to get along with, but Howard seemed to be the yin to her yang. He wasn't a pushover by any means, but up until this point, he seemed to know how to handle her.

Juliette hoped they were in there working out their problems. Her mother may not have been lucky in love, but Howard was good for her. They were good for each other. And with Howard there, Guinevere might be distracted enough to forget about giving Juliette the inquisition over spending time with Jude tonight.

Juliette's defenses were low right now. Her emotions were probably written all over her face. Emotions of love and confusion and…she didn't know what.

If she'd been confused before she left the house this evening, her head was spinning now.

Jude said he still loved her. That he'd never stopped loving her. She loved him. But what were they supposed to do when even though they wanted each other, they seemed to want completely different things in life?

It seemed like an impossible situation.

Making love to him had been the equivalent of ripping open a wound that had scarred over without healing. She could see that now. After the fact. Now that she sat here aching and raw. More than ever it seemed as though he was going to risk everything and ride one more year.

She'd had to grit her teeth to keep from throwing down the ultimatum, *If you love me you won't go.*

She hadn't said it because she shouldn't have to say

it. If he loved her he wouldn't go; he wouldn't take the risk and put himself in danger. It should be that simple.

But he did love her and she loved him. At least they had that…even though it complicated the situation.

When it came down to it, she loved him so much that she wouldn't force him into a situation he wouldn't choose of his own volition.

"Thanks for driving me home," she said.

He answered her with a kiss, slow and sweet. And she kissed him back trying to memorize this moment in case it was the last time. Because once she got out of his truck, it *should* be the last time—until they both figured out what they wanted and knew they were on the same page.

"I need to go, before my mother starts flicking the porch lights on and off."

Jude laughed and leaned his head back against the headrest, running his hand through his hair. "Remember how she used to do that? She couldn't stand the thought of us being alone out here in my truck."

"She was so concerned about what the neighbors would think," Juliette said, the memory bringing a sad smile to her lips. "Never mind that her flashing the lights was like a neon sign that made everyone look."

They laughed again and Jude leaned in and kissed her one more time. Then he pulled back just enough to lean his forehead against hers, his palm still cupping her cheek. He stroked her jawline for a moment before he said, "I guess we should say good-night. But I don't want to say good-night. I want to share your bed. I want your face to be the last thing I see before I close my eyes and the first thing I see when I wake up with you in the morning."

The thought awakened her hunger for him all over again.

"Guinevere would love that, wouldn't she?" The question was more of a reminder to herself than it was meant for him.

"And I'm worried that once you get out of this truck, everything between us is going to change," he confessed.

"Well, I think I made it clear how you could make sure everything ended up in your favor," she answered. "At least as far as I'm concerned."

"I know." He scrubbed his hand over his eyes. "Don't give up on me. Let me work on it, okay? I may still have some tricks up my sleeve."

She nodded.

"You're still going to be my date to the homecoming dance, right?" he said.

"I don't know. You never asked me to be your date."

He smiled and pushed a strand of hair out of her eyes. "I'm asking you now. Juliette Lowell, will you go to the homecoming dance with me?"

She kissed him. "I'd love to go to the homecoming dance with you."

"I'm getting you a corsage," he said as he opened his car door.

"What? Wait. Where are you going?" Juliette asked.

He unbuckled his seat belt. "I'm walking you to the door."

She unbuckled her seat belt, but stayed put, smiling

at the idea of a corsage, letting him be the gentleman and open her car door. He took her hand and helped her out, pulling her into his arms for one more kiss.

"You need to get inside, before I get us both in trouble," he said into her lips.

"My dress is blue," she said.

His brows furrowed and he glanced down between them. "No, it's not, it's pink."

"My homecoming dress. It's blue."

His eyes flashed. "Okay. Noted."

He slipped an arm around her waist and held her tight against his side as he walked her up to the porch. He was just leaning in for one last kiss when the door opened.

"Is that you, Juliette?" It was Howard. Even so, the two of them flinched apart.

"Hi, Howard. Yes, it's me. I'm glad you're here. How's my mother?"

Howard regarded Jude critically. "She's fine. Fine. Everything is just fine. No worries here. She didn't want to leave until you got home, and I wanted to meet your young man. I understand he's quite a local celebrity. Howard Albright," he said as he extended his hand to Jude.

Jude met his grip. "Jude Campbell, sir. It's nice to meet you."

"Yes. Yes. Very nice to meet you. Come inside, both of you. I brought your mother her favorite rum cake. Come in and have a piece with us."

Jude hung back. "Thanks for the offer, but—"

"Nonsense," Howard said. "It'll take fifteen minutes. Come in. I've already got the coffee brewing."

Juliette could smell the coffee when she stepped into the foyer. It smelled good. One of Howard's many attributes was that he knew how to brew the perfect cup of joe. Juliette turned back to Jude. "You might as well come in. When Howard gets his mind made up, there's no talking him out of it."

She smiled at Jude, hoping that he understood she was humoring the older man.

"Well, since you put it that way…" Jude said.

Howard had already disappeared inside the house. Juliette hung back in the foyer while Jude stepped inside and shut the door. Franklin finally realized she was home, and he moseyed in to meet her. Looking sleepy, the red-and-white dog dropped down and stretched his front paws out in front of him and kept his rear end up in the air. He threw back his furry little head and howled his hello.

Juliette bent down and stroked his velvety ear. "Hi, buddy. Are you glad I'm home? I missed you."

The little dog turned his attention to Jude and howled again. This time the modulated yowl sounded like a yodel. Jude squatted down and gave the little guy some strokes. The dog thanked him with a lick on the nose. "Whoa there," he said as he stood up. "We don't know each other that well. If we did you would know I don't kiss on the first date."

"Oh, yeah?" Juliette said. "That's not what I hear."

Her right eyebrow shot up. Jude pulled her into his arms again.

"Juliette, do you want some cake?" Guinevere called. "I'm plating it now."

It was as if the woman had some sort of radar or uncanny sixth sense that told her the most inopportune moments to insert herself. But the thing was, they weren't eighteen anymore. If she wanted to stand in the foyer of her own home and kiss a guy that her mother *still* didn't approve of, she would do it. Except that she'd promised herself she wouldn't kiss Jude again once she'd gotten out of the truck.

Okay, make that once he'd left the house.

Juliette didn't answer her mother about the cake. Instead, she leaned in and tasted Jude's lips again. She just couldn't get enough.

"Juliette, cake?" Guinevere insisted.

"Yes, cake. Two pieces, please. One for me, one for Jude. And coffee for both of us. Thank you." She kissed him again.

"Come on," Jude said.

They walked into the kitchen, squinting into the bright light.

Guinevere made a point of looking at the clock. "It's rather late, don't you think?"

"It's ten thirty," Juliette answered. "I'm a grown woman. I can stay out as late as I choose."

Guinevere *harrumphed* and carefully slid a piece of rum cake onto a plate.

"So, young man," Howard said. "You're dating my daughter? Technically, she might be my stepdaughter, but she's the daughter I've always wanted and I'd like to know your intentions."

It should've rankled Juliette. Did Howard think she was sixteen?

She sighed silently to herself.

But he was so earnest—not gruff in the least, but truly concerned for her well-being—that she simply turned to Jude and gave him the big eyes. Actually, she was interested in hearing what he would say being put on the spot like this.

Guinevere remained uncharacteristically quiet as Jude opened up and told Howard the truth—that he was at a crossroads in his life. He told him about winning the championship and his struggles with injuries the following year. He told him about Copenhagen and how they were still trying to come to a meeting of the minds and they would finalize things when they met at the Bull Riding Expo in Vegas the week of the twenty-third. He told him about his idea of opening a bull riding school in Celebration—something with a charitable mission.

Juliette was heartened at how open and forthright Jude was with this man he'd just met. She shouldn't have been surprised, because for as long as she'd known Jude, he'd always been a *what you see is what you get* kind of guy.

She was just as surprised by the way Howard opened up.

"I understand where you're coming from, son," he said. "Life will throw you a curveball once in a while. You just have to roll with it and not give up. Even at my age—and I've been in business for a long time— I'm in the midst of a business crisis as we speak. I don't mind sharing it with you because maybe you can learn something."

He glanced at Guinevere and smiled knowingly.

"Oh, Howard, I don't understand why you feel the need to air our private business."

But that was the end of her protest. She turned her attention to her plate, forked up a bite of cake and chewed it slowly as Howard continued.

"It seems I've hit a financial setback, but I'm not throwing my hands up. When something's important, you work hard and you protect it. You persevere, because in the end it comes down to a battle between you and defeat. If you want it bad enough you will win. I've been working extra hours to court a new client that could make or break me. And it's not going to break me. I'll tell you that right now.

"I'm going to digress for a moment. Juliette, your mother has been worried because I've been working extra hours. I should've told her what was going on, but I didn't. I didn't want to worry her. But I want you to know everything is fine. I would never do anything to hurt your mother. She's my pride and joy."

Guinevere's face softened and she looked downright smitten. Juliette hadn't seen her mother look like that since—well, since before Juliette's father had passed away.

"I'm telling you both this because, Jude, I expect nothing less from you where Juliette is concerned. You seem to be a nice, responsible young man and you seem to be crazy about our daughter. I get the feeling she's crazy about you. And I have to say, if I were in the financial position to invest in your bull riding school, I just might do it. In fact, give me a few months to get back on solid footing and send me a proposal and we'll see what I can do."

Because Howard was just that kind of man. Honest, steadfast and generous.

For the first time in the history of Jude and Juliette, Guinevere hadn't snarled at Jude as she said good-night and went home with Howard, leaving the two of them alone.

It was a moment Juliette had longed for. It only added to her confusion.

It would've been so easy to ask Jude to stay the night. It would've been like heaven waking up in his arms, but even though the universe had shifted and the world had tipped on its axis with her mother's apparent acquiescence, Juliette knew until Jude made his final verdict in Vegas on October 23, she needed to slow things way down and protect her heart. She needed to put some solid distance between them starting now.

On the night of the homecoming parade, barbecue and football game, Juliette had arranged to meet Jude at Celebration's Central Park, at the point where the parade was supposed to start.

In a vindicating turn of events, an alumnus who could not attend the reunion had donated twenty-five hundred dollars for the class gift. Two and a half times the amount they'd hoped to raise via that crazy talent show. With that, low ticket sales and the general lack of enthusiasm over revisiting adolescent humiliation, Marilyn and Marcy had reluctantly canceled the show.

There couldn't have been a better note on which to kick off the reunion and homecoming activities.

Juliette was already at the park when Jude arrived for the parade. Her shop was right across the street. It was just as well he hadn't suggested they meet up. She hadn't returned his texts and he got the feeling she could use some space.

Even so, it hadn't stopped him from sending flowers to her shop today.

He caught her eye as he walked up to the candy-apple-red 1962 Mustang convertible that sported a sign that said Grand Marshals—Jude Campbell and Juliette Lowell—Class of 2007.

"Thanks for the roses," she said quietly. "They're gorgeous. You didn't have to do that."

"But I wanted to do that."

He wished he could do so much more. He wished he could send a dozen roses for every day they'd been apart, but if their night together had scared her, a daily barrage of roses might send her running.

He had, however, included a message with the flowers: "Don't give up on me."

She looked up into his eyes and he had to resist the urge to bend down and kiss her. Too bad they had to spend the evening here in the midst of so many people. He was usually a sociable guy, but not knowing how much longer he would stay in Celebration made him want to spend as much time with her as possible.

As the parade organizers called for everyone to take their places, Jude and Juliette greeted their driver. Jude helped Juliette into the car and helped her adjust the hem of her long red dress so that he didn't step on it as he got into the car. It reminded him of when they had ridden in the homecoming parade ten years ago, the night that they were crowned king and queen.

Things had been a lot simpler back then.

On second thought, his teenage problems, his differences with his dad, hadn't been simple at all, just *different*. He thought about what Howard had said the night of their discussion.

When something's important, you work hard and you protect it. You persevere, because in the end it comes down to a battle between you and defeat. If you want it bad enough you will win.

The man was right. Jude's own belief coupled with Howard's philosophy were making it so hard to not compete this last season. It didn't hurt that today had been a good day with no headaches and minimal body aches.

When a pro bull rider did his job right, things usually didn't go wrong. It was a contest of strength, endurance and wills. Man against beast. If the cowboy did what he was supposed to do—commanded the bull for eight seconds—everything was fine. Most of the time that's how it went down, even if the rider got thrown before the full ride; with the help of the rodeo clown, who took his own life in his hands diverting the attention of the angry three-thousand-pound beast, the rider usually had time to pick himself up and get out of danger. But when things went wrong, it could be catastrophic. Jude had just gotten unlucky.

Next year could be his year.

The car began moving forward, making a slow crawl down Main Street. As they waved to the cheering crowd, which had gathered on either side of the street, Jude said, "Did you hear that Tony and Janet Darcy had the baby? He called me today and told me the good news. He asked if I could fill in for him as advisor of the rodeo club while he's out on family leave."

Juliette's eyes widened. "Are you going to do it? That means you'd have to stay in Celebration, though. Right?"

Jude shrugged. "I don't know. I'll have to see how things work out. He says I'll need to go to the county to get approved to be a permanent volunteer. So I don't know. We'll see. While I had him on the phone, I told him that I was thinking about starting a bull riding school. I asked him if he was interested in being part of it."

"What did he say?"

"He said he might be able to do something part-time, but with the new baby, he's not in a position to invest or leave his job at the high school. So then I started thinking that if I sold a portion of the land, I might have enough to cover start-up costs."

"Are you serious? Do you think that could actually happen?"

Juliette's eyes were so big and so full of hope, he realized he might've given her the wrong impression. He was just dreaming out loud, bouncing ideas off her like he always used to do. He was just musing, trying the idea on for size.

"I don't know if that's going to happen. I'd be in

much better financial shape if I did the circuit for another year. That way, Copenhagen might continue my sponsorship. When I talked to Bob today, he said if I will ride another year, he will try to get them to move the sponsorship to the bull riding school."

Juliette turned away and waved to people who were on the side of the street closest to her. When she looked back at him she seemed a little distant.

"Well, I have some news of my own. Lucy and I met with an attorney today. I've accepted her offer to buy Weddings by Juliette. The attorney is drawing up the papers and we should finalize everything early next week, if not sooner."

Chapter Ten

For the past decade, Jude had been so focused on making it to the top of his career, he hadn't had time to think about concrete steps to the next path of his life. Not yet. It didn't seem possible that he was *there* yet.

He was aware that his career as a bull rider was short-lived, and at twenty-eight, he could see the PBR sun beginning to set on the horizon. But the horizon had seemed so far away. When he'd won the world championship, retiring had been the last thing on his mind. He'd kept himself in top physical shape, saved part of every single cash prize he'd won and royalty he'd earned, and he'd had a rough idea that he'd like to parlay his experience into a school that taught young cowboys and cowgirls proper technique. What he hadn't planned for was for his career to be cut short and for medical bills to eat up his savings.

When it came to his professional life, he'd never been faced with choices beyond what bull to ride and which shade of green he preferred for the On-Off Shirt—moss green over Kelly green. That's why the decision of whether or not to retire early was a tough one.

The clock was ticking and he had to figure it out.

But he did need to figure out what he was going to do and just do it. Quit talking about it, quit going back and forth weighing options and make a decision. The first step in that direction was to talk to Ethan about the land. Last night at the game, his brother had mentioned that he had an idea he wanted to run by him. Jude was open for anything right now. Plus, he figured it would be as good a time as any to tell him he was considering putting his property on the market. Even though Ethan had said it wasn't in his budget to buy it, he still owed it to his brother to give him first right of refusal for this new option.

Jude parked his truck in Ethan's driveway. He went up to the door and knocked. It felt odd knocking after spending more than half of his life walking right into the place. If Ethan wasn't married to Chelsea, he might've still walked in unannounced, but now that Chelsea had made Ethan an honest man, he figured he owed them the common courtesy.

The thought made him smile because he couldn't remember a time when his older brother had not been an honest man. They were as different as night and day, as chocolate and vanilla, as jalapeños and green peppers.

Chelsea answered the door and greeted him with a hug.

"Hello, Jude. Ethan is in the kitchen. He just finished lunch. Are you hungry?"

"No, thanks, Chelsea. I'm fine. I just need to talk to my brother."

He loved his sister-in-law's warmth. She seemed like she'd been part of the family forever. She'd done wonders for his brother. He'd never seen Ethan this happy. As he walked past the living room, he glanced at the couch where Juliette had been sitting the other night, as if he expected to see her there. Of course, the room was empty. He wondered if he and Juliette would ever find the same kind of happiness his brother and Chelsea had found. Things just seemed to flow so naturally for them. But they hadn't been without their struggles. Relationships took effort and a strong foundation based on both partners wanting the same things in life.

Even though he wasn't giving up on the two of them, it seemed like he and Juliette just couldn't get to common ground. What made it worse was that each of them was at crossroads and they couldn't seem to meet in the middle.

She was selling her business to Lucy. She had no idea what she wanted to do, except that she knew she didn't want to spend a year on the road with him. The rational part of him understood that she had a hard time watching him ride; she didn't want to see him get hurt. All that aside, he couldn't blame her for not wanting to put her life on hold for a year. He didn't expect her to. But another part of Jude wished that she would give just a couple of inches. Maybe spend a couple of weeks with him as he competed. She'd indicated she might want to go into business with him. He tried to make her see that the best place for her to learn the ins and outs of that business was to get a good taste of what the kids who would be their clients would be learning from them. Sure, she'd been a barrel racer in high school, but that was longer ago than either of them wanted to admit.

When Jude entered the kitchen, Ethan was standing at the sink rinsing dishes and loading them into the dishwasher.

"I didn't realize my brother could be domesticated, Chelsea," Jude said.

"He is absolutely wonderful in every single regard exactly as he is." Chelsea walked up behind Ethan and put her arms around his middle and gave him a squeeze. Watching them made him long for Juliette.

Jude made a sound of mock disgust. It came out sounding feral.

"Yeah, not all of us are wild and untamable," Ethan said. He dried his hands on a dish towel.

"Oh, I don't know, Ethan," said Chelsea. "I think there's hope for your little brother. He and Juliette looked adorable at the parade yesterday. I'm sorry I didn't get a chance to see you at the game last night, except from afar when you were out on the field crowning the new homecoming king and queen. Did you have fun last night?"

"It was a busy night." Jude tried to keep his voice light as he skirted the question.

Because actually, they hadn't had a very good time.

Or at least he hadn't. Not with Juliette, anyway. She had become more and more aloof as the night went on.

After the parade, Juliette had been distant to the point that it almost seemed as if she was avoiding him. He'd been replaying the night in his head trying to figure out what he'd done to offend her.

Maybe he'd shared too much as they rode in the parade. In retrospect, he wondered if he should've kept his thoughts and musings closer to the chest. It seemed natural to tell her about how he'd shared his plans with Tony Darcy. She'd seemed jazzed about Tony asking him to fill in as the rodeo club sponsor. When he'd backtracked after she'd asked him if he was actually considering it, he thought he'd seen disappointment in her eyes. She'd gotten so quiet. He hadn't taken offense when she'd given him clipped, one- or two-word answers when he'd asked her for more details about the deal with Lucy. The transaction wasn't final and Lucy hadn't yet announced that she was merging Juliette's business with the Campbell Wedding Barn. He figured it wasn't really a good place to get into the nitty-gritty.

After the parade, they'd eaten the barbecue with a group of former classmates. However, when they'd gone to the football game, they had gotten separated and didn't meet up again until halftime when they were on the field to help crown this year's new homecoming king and queen. By that time, he knew for a fact she was avoiding him.

He'd asked her if she was okay. She'd said she was. At least he'd had the foresight to confirm that they still had a date for the dance tonight. She'd said, *Of course*. He'd told her he'd pick her up at six o'clock this evening.

After that, she'd said a quick good-night and had disappeared into the crowd. Jude had let her go. Maybe it wasn't about him at all. Maybe she needed to process her feelings about selling her business. The deal had happened fast. It might have turned into a case of *be careful what you wish for*.

"Is someone taking pictures for you tonight?" Chelsea asked. "Because if you don't have a photographer, I'm happy to volunteer."

"Thanks for the offer," he said. "I'm sure there will be plenty of cameras."

"I hope so," she said. "It sounds like so much fun. We didn't have a homecoming dance where I went to school in London."

"Baby, when my class reunion rolls around again, I'll take you to the dance," Ethan said. He pulled her into his arms and kissed her.

"Okay, you two. Get a room. Or better yet, Ethan, you come with me on a walkabout."

Ethan's part of the property was on one edge of the Campbell property and Jude's was on the opposite side. The stretch that their sister owned ran right down the middle.

"Feel like walking down to the lake?" Jude asked.

It was a little over a third of a mile from one edge of the property to the other. It would give them a good chance to talk. Being outside, walking the land, would feel like neutral territory.

They left Ethan's house through the back door and

started across the field that was his backyard. They walked in silence for about five minutes when Jude's phone rang. He pulled it from his pocket and looked at it.

"Sorry, man, I've got to take this. It's my agent."

"No problem," Ethan said.

Jude picked up the call. "Bob. What's up?"

"Jude, are you ready for this? Hold on to your hat. I've got some good news."

"Yeah? Let's hear it."

"I heard back from Clive Curtis over at Copenhagen. They say if you ride one more year they will keep the On-Off clothing line alive through the term of your sponsorship contract. How 'bout that? I'd say it couldn't have gone better."

For all intents and purposes, it was the best possible scenario. If he had a good run next year, he would be sitting on top of the world. It was the sign he'd been looking for, the tipping point to make his decision.

Jude should've been ready to celebrate, but he wasn't.

"What about the charitable donation?"

"No. They're dropping that this year. But don't you think that's kind of run its course, anyway?"

"No. I don't think it's run its course. I won't give that up to corporate greed. Go back and tell them that's a deal breaker."

Bob was silent for several beats. "Okay, yeah. Don't lose the war because you want to win this battle," he said. "You mull it over. We'll talk about it more next week in Vegas."

Jude ended the call and felt his brother's expectant gaze on him.

"Did you get some news?" Ethan asked.

"I guess you could call it that," Jude said. "They weren't the terms I wanted. I need Bob to go back and try again."

Ethan nodded. "Speaking of terms, I need to talk to you about something. I crunched some numbers after we talked. I tried to come up with a fair offer for your part of the land, but I just couldn't make it work. I have to be conservative. I need to make sure I don't expand the Triple C too fast. Plus, Chelsea and I are talking about starting a family pretty soon. Babies are expensive."

No surprise that they were looking to grow their family.

"I've done some number crunching of my own," Jude said. "It looks like I don't have a choice. I need to sell half my land. Just half, though. I'm going to keep the rest. The part with the cabin on it. With the money from the sale, and it looks like Copenhagen is willing to extend the On-Off gig for another season, I think I'll have the capital I need to come back to Celebration and open the riding school."

"Where does the PBR season fit into that?"

Jude shrugged. "Depends on how fast the property sells and what I get for it. Best case is it sells straightaway and I can retire this year. Worst case is it doesn't sell. Then I'll have no choice but to go one more season. Of course, even better scenario is that it sells and I ride."

And win. And don't kill myself or end up paralyzed in the process.

"Have you ever thought about just getting an ordinary job like the rest of us schmoes?" Ethan asked.

"Of course I have. I just can't make the kind of money I would with the sponsorship, the clothing line and winnings."

Ethan nodded again. "I have a proposition for you. Will you keep an open mind?"

"Sure."

"Do you have a location for the school in mind?" Ethan asked.

"I have a couple of ideas, but I haven't had a chance to make any inquiries. I was going to do that the week before I leave for Vegas."

They were approaching the lake. The cabin loomed off to the right like a specter. Even though he'd spent two nights there since Juliette had been there, every time he came near it, he thought of her.

He stayed quiet, focusing on what Ethan was saying, willing himself not to think of her.

"How would you feel about opening a riding school as part of Triple C Ranch? I could put you on the payroll. I'll make it worth your while if you'll help out with the breeding arm of the business. I just had a foreman quit on me. I figure I might as well hire family rather than bring in someone else. The salary is not enough money to make you rich and the job won't make you famous, but I figure I can afford to pay you in the 50K range. You could use the barn and riding ring east of the stables to get started and add equipment as you can afford it. With a steady job, you might even qualify for a business loan to help you get up to speed faster. The folks at the bank can help you with that. I hope this will make it possible for you to hang on to your land."

Jude's body went numb. He had to give himself a mental shake. It was a generous offer. After the initial aversion to the idea of being confined to the sameness of a workaday job where he had to report to someone— even if that someone was his brother—he had to stop himself from asking, *What's the catch?*

With their dad there had always been a catch. Or hell to pay.

But Ethan was not their dad.

"You would do that for me?" Jude asked quietly.

"Hell, yeah, I would. That's what family is for. Jude, there's no shame in asking for help. God knows I needed a lot of help when I went through my dark night."

"I wasn't there for you when you were going through your crap."

"It's okay. You've been battling your own demons. Consider this me paying it forward."

"You really are too good, aren't you?" Jude said.

"No. I'm not. Because I want something from you."

Ah, the catch.

"What?"

"I want you to lose the chip on your shoulder. I want you to stop pushing people away, acting like you're alone in this world. Cut yourself a break and let me give you a hand up." Ethan smiled, but there was an edge to the look in his eyes. It said even though he was being nice, he meant business. "Cut us all a damn break and get over yourself. If you let Juliette get away this time, you deserve to be miserable."

A dry hiccup of a laugh escaped from the back of Jude's throat.

"Well, there you go," Jude said. "If your own brother can't tell you to get over yourself, who can?"

In his experience, family—his folks mostly—had never been there for him. His dad had made him feel like a burden and managed to turn everything into a battle of wits. His mom had been her husband's subservient enabler, simply trying to preempt anything that might make her alcoholic husband explode.

But since Ethan's wedding, since reconnecting with him and talking to Lucy regularly via text and semiweekly phone calls, he could now see that his brother and sister—and Juliette—were all the family he'd ever needed.

He'd allowed his animosity toward his father and the hurt Donovan Campbell had caused to keep him from home.

He had been such a bastard.

After he'd beaten up Jude over the mistake with the books, Jude had left. They'd never really talked again and three months later, his dad was dead.

Before that, Jude had brought Glori home, which had been a mistake in itself. He had no business saying yes to the woman when she'd asked him to marry her. She had proposed and he'd wanted something—anything— to blunt the pain of losing Juliette.

He'd called his mom to see if he could come by the house and introduce her, but his mom had said it was still too soon, his father was still simmering…or maybe she'd said it wasn't a good time…or some other thinly veiled excuse. At the time, Jude had taken it personally, but now, all of a sudden, the slow dawning realization hit him that the alcohol had made his dad a ticking time bomb. Jude and all his bright shiny dreams—the very dreams that his father had never been able to achieve— had been the spark that had lit the fuse. His dad had died drunk behind the wheel and had essentially taken their mother with him. She'd survived the crash but had ended up a paraplegic and had died ten months later.

His dad had died a disgrace. He'd killed himself before Jude had the chance to prove him wrong.

And Jude still felt like he couldn't measure up. That was some screwed-up thinking. If only it were easy to put it to rest.

"I still have to go to this Expo in Las Vegas next week. I'm contractually bound by my Copenhagen contract. It's my last obligation."

Ethan nodded. "Why don't you take some time to think it over and if you want the job you can start when you get back from the Expo?"

The thought of reporting to the same job, confined to the same place day in and day out, after having his freedom—reporting to no one but the folks at the rodeo check-in desk and the bull in the chute—made him chafe.

Ethan would be his boss. Of course Jude would strive to do a good job and Ethan was not a hard-ass like their father…

Even though Ethan's offer made so much sense,

would Jude really be able to settle down into so much normal? Or would he end up spontaneously combusting and ruining his relationships with Ethan, Lucy…and Juliette? The same way he and his father had torched their relationship?

Maybe for the sake of preserving the relationships he'd forged with Ethan and Lucy, he'd do everyone a favor by competing one more year.

"I can't believe I just bought your business." In the elevator of the office of her attorney, Seth Ryan, Lucy clapped her hands like a child who had just discovered the prize at the bottom of the cereal box.

Juliette looked at the check in her hand. She counted the zeros following the rather large prime number. "I can't believe you just handed me a check for this much money. I can't believe you had the savings for this much money. This is insane."

It shouldn't have come as a surprise. Juliette knew the wedding business was lucrative. She tucked the check into her purse and the two women walked arm in arm out of the lobby onto Main Street.

"I know you have plans with my brother tonight," Lucy said. "But let's go get a glass of champagne to celebrate. Tori and Chelsea want us to meet them at the bar at Café St. Germaine."

Juliette's insides took a long, slow roll at the mention of Jude. She hated herself for it. He was leaving. He may not know it yet, but Juliette could see the warning signs. If she could be any more invested than she already was, she needed to protect her heart. It had become crystal clear last night at the parade. By this point, if Jude couldn't say he was staying, there was a very good chance he was leaving. And she would not follow him. She wished he hadn't even brought up Tony Darcy's invitation to be the advisor for the rodeo club while he was out on family leave.

The sisters were waiting at a high table in the bar with an iced bottle of Veuve Clicquot and a glass of sparkling cider for Lucy since the expectant mother wasn't drinking alcohol.

They looked stunning—Tori in a black-and-white shift dress with opaque black tights and ankle boots; Chelsea in an orange-and-pink tunic with leggings and boots. Their outfits were from Tori's latest collection. When Chelsea and Juliette had been in college, Tori had let them borrow liberally from her samples. Since they were sample sizes, it gave Juliette plenty of inspiration to stay fit. Lucky for her, Tori's signature style flattered curvy girls.

"Is it done?" Chelsea asked.

"It's done!" Lucy and Juliette said in unison.

It seemed surreal to think that she had just divested herself of what had been her entire post-college life. Of course, that meant Tabatha was part of the bargain, too. Lucy would inherit the queen of the bridezillas. But Juliette didn't have the heart to simply throw Lucy to the wolves, even though Lucy had dealt with her share of bridezillas. Ah, well, they still had a couple of weeks before Tabatha's wedding. In the meantime, Juliette decided she would try to relax a little and figure out what was next.

Tori poured the champagne and the Ashford Alden sisters raised their glasses in a toast to the newly minted transaction.

"This one is for Juliette," said Chelsea. "To happiness and good health, and good riddance to bridezillas."

"And one for Lucy," echoed Tori. "May you keep the bridezillas on a tight leash and live happily ever after."

They all laughed.

"The only thing standing between my eternal happiness is a trip to the ladies' room," said Lucy. "Why did no one warn me that pregnancy shrinks your bladder? Would anyone care to come along?"

"I will," said Chelsea.

The two were off, leaving Tori and Juliette alone with the champagne.

"So, tell me, Jules—you're really and truly unencumbered these days? No job? No Jude?"

Juliette's stomach did that clinch-roll thing again. It felt like taking a drop on a kiddie roller coaster. Only this was not child's play. She needed to shore up her defenses.

But she couldn't help wondering how Tori knew that there was *no Jude*. Or better yet, what intel Tori might have overheard at the Campbell dinner table to make her so sure Jude wasn't in the picture. Maybe Jude had finally made a decision.

"No job. The only man in my life is my corgi, Franklin. Why do you ask?"

"Because I'd like to offer you a job. How would you feel about moving to London and heading up the brandnew bridal division of Tori Ashford Alden Designs?

With your knowledge of the American bridal industry and your eye for design, you are just the person I've been looking for."

Chapter Eleven

He'd talked about himself too much last night. Tonight would be fun, Jude vowed as he traversed Juliette's porch steps, a corsage of white tea roses in hand.

Nothing heavy.

Nothing about Ethan's offer and his own trepidations.

Tonight would be about them.

He had bought a brand-new pair of dark blue jeans and a white shirt. But at the last minute, he had scrapped the jeans for the khakis that he'd worn the other night. He'd paired them with a suit jacket and blue tie since Juliette had mentioned that her dress would be blue. He wanted her to see that he had made an effort. He had. And it had been for her. Getting dressed up like this had never been his gig. She knew him well enough to know that.

He knocked on the door and waited for her to answer, feeling as nervous as if this was their first date. In some ways it was, because he wanted a clean slate, wanted to reset the relationship and start over.

She took his breath away when she answered the door. "Hi," she said. Her eyes widened. "Look at you. You clean up nicely."

Juliette was one of those women who was equally comfortable in blue jeans and fussy formalwear. Still, he couldn't remember her ever looking more beautiful than she did tonight.

She'd twisted her hair up off her shoulders so that it framed her gorgeous face. She was wearing a blue cocktail dress that showed off her curves and tempted him to reach in and pull her to him.

But he didn't.

Instead, he focused on the sexy, strappy silver sandals she wore and how they elongated her tanned legs. They made her stand nearly at eye level with him. For a moment he was rendered speechless.

"Hey," he finally said.

"Ready to go?" she asked.

As she pulled the door shut, he noticed that she had her purse, an evening wrap and a small white box at the ready. No need for them to go inside. He held up the medium-size box that contained her corsage.

"I brought you this." He opened the plastic box and took out the flowers. They were on an elastic band so she could slip them on her wrist. When he'd taken her to the dances in high school, he'd always gotten the kind of flower that was pinned on the dress, but the florist had suggested that a corsage worn on the wrist might be more practical. Since he planned to hold her close when they danced, she was probably right. This way he wouldn't crush her flowers.

"It's beautiful, Jude. Thank you."

She opened the small white box and took out a single white rosebud. It was similar to her corsage. His first thought was *great minds*. But then he realized that the florist had probably clued her into the color and type of flower of the corsage he had ordered for her.

It was nice how they matched. It looked like they belonged together.

After she pinned the boutonniere onto his lapel, he offered her his arm and they made their way to the truck. After he'd left Ethan, he'd washed the truck and cleaned up the inside. He opened the door and helped her into the cab. He wasn't a fancy person. In fact, beyond their dinner date the other night, he couldn't remember the last time he'd gotten dressed up. Their high school graduation, maybe? No. He'd worn jeans and boots under his graduation gown. Maybe it had been their prom? Whatever the occasion, Juliette had undoubtedly been there.

It was a short drive to the Campbell Wedding Barn. Even though the drive had been mostly silent, they arrived before the silence could get awkward.

Jude parked. He was glad that she waited for him to walk around and open her door and help her out. It made it seem more like a date—that even though things might have been a little strained these past couple of days, they enjoyed each other's company and wanted to be together, rather than simply going to the dance together because being together was an old habit that neither of them had really and truly kicked. The truth was he did want to be with her.

Could he ever get to the point where his need to be with her outweighed his need to prove his father wrong? Or maybe he was trying to prove himself wrong?

He wasn't going to ruin the night by being in his head too much.

As they walked up the mulch path from the gravel parking lot to the barn, it dawned on him that maybe this battle he'd been waging had only been against himself. Maybe it was time to make peace with himself.

He put his hand on the small of Juliette's back as they approached the barn. When they entered, they were greeted by festive music played by a live band, the aroma of steaks grilling somewhere outside the open side doors and the chatter of people who were already having a great time.

After the football game, he had helped with the decorating—mostly moving heavy objects like tables and chairs. He'd signed up to help, but when he'd turned up, he'd had ulterior motives, hoping to find Juliette there, but she'd been conspicuously absent.

Someone had done a whole lot more to the place, stringing market lights and small white twinkle lights across the room, setting up round tables with white tablecloths, candles and centerpieces, and adding strategically placed up-lighting around the space. The barn looked less like a barn and more like a rustic, urban restaurant. Like something you might find in Houston or Dallas rather than in the small town of Celebration.

"It looks so nice in here," Juliette said. "I helped out before the parade yesterday, and it was taking shape, but it didn't look anywhere near this good. Somebody obviously went above and beyond."

"That would be me," said Marcy, who had appeared out of nowhere.

Of course it was. Did the woman sleep?

"The place looks great, Marcy," said Juliette. "Thanks for all your hard work. I hope there's no hard feelings over the talent show."

Marcy's toothy smile was as forced as a bad sitcom conflict. "Yes, well, I suppose everything worked out for the best. We wouldn't want to force anyone to do anything she didn't want to do, would we? Did you say you helped decorate yesterday? I didn't see you here."

"Yes, I was here before the parade."

Marcy looked at her dubiously. "*Huh.* I was here then. I must've missed you."

She turned to Jude. "I definitely saw you here after the game. I don't know what we would've done without your strong muscles, moving all those chairs and tables. Thanks so much for your help."

The shift in Marcy's demeanor when she spoke to him was vast and a little embarrassing. He'd only hefted some things around. It wasn't as if he had come up with the decorating scheme—or even implemented it.

"Save me a dance, Jude." It wasn't a request. It was a command.

What happened to not forcing anyone to do anything they didn't want to do?

Marcy flagged down someone else, breaking into a cheerleader *squee* and hugging a woman he didn't recognize.

"This might be a very long night," said Juliette.

"Not if I have anything to say about it. I didn't put on khakis and a tie to have a bad time." He flashed her his most winning smile. "You just wait."

She laughed. For the first time that night she seemed more herself.

A few steps inside the door was a table with name tags that had their yearbook pictures on them. They waited in line behind several people who stopped to laugh at their own photos and poke fun at their friends' pictures.

"No one can accuse us of being a stylish group, can they?" he said as he and Juliette waited their turn.

"Oh, I don't know, we thought we were pretty snazzy back in the day. That was the era of headbands, baby doll dresses and low-slung jeans with midriffs."

"How could I forget the low-slung jeans and midriffs?" he said. "All I remember is that you always looked mighty fine. You were the exception to the unstylish rule."

"There you go with the flattery again."

When they finally made it to the table, they had just grabbed their own name tags when Lucy appeared next to them. "Hey, you guys. I'm so glad I found you. You two look cute. Here, let me take your picture. I promised Chelsea I would snap some shots because knowing you two, you'd forget. Stand right over there."

They cleared the name tag table so they wouldn't hold up the line and keep others from picking up theirs. God knew it was moving slowly enough just with the people stopping to gawk at the pictures.

"Jude, put your arm around her. Juliette, put your hand up on his chest so we can see your corsage. Prom pose! Even if this is homecoming, do a prom pose. It's good for all occasions."

Lucy babbled on as she snapped some shots with the camera on her cell phone. Since she was three years younger than Jude and Juliette, she wasn't attending the reunion as a guest. She was actually working since she was the venue manager on duty that night. But it would be fun to hang out with her for a little bit, since she always added a special spark of levity.

"Oh, these are cute," she said as she scrolled through the pictures. "Look. I really like this one. You two are ridiculously adorable."

They huddled together looking at the shots Lucy had snapped. They did look good together. But more important, they were good together. They were good for each other.

"Everything looks great, huh?" Lucy cooed. "I was so glad when Marcy and Marilyn asked about holding the reunion here. I wouldn't mind doing more nonwedding business here at the barn. Of course, that is going to be more challenging thanks to everything that's just happened."

In all her pregnant glory, Lucy looked as if she was about to bubble over.

"Jules told you the good news, didn't she?" she said, looking back and forth between them.

"She told me you wanted to buy her business," Jude said. "I take it that everything is going well in that department?"

Lucy's mouth fell open. "Juliette, didn't you tell your boyfriend the good news?"

He might have worried about Lucy making things uncomfortable with labels like "boyfriend," but Juliette knew as well as he did that's just how Lucy was. She meant no harm by it.

"What's the good news?" he asked.

"Lucy and I closed on the sale today," Juliette said. She didn't look quite as overjoyed as Lucy did.

"Yes, you are standing in the official new home of Weddings by Juliette."

He looked from Lucy to Juliette. "Seriously? It's official? That fast?"

"That fast," Lucy said. "I think we should have another glass of champagne to celebrate. Do they have champagne at this shindig? If not, I have some in my office. Of course, mine will be club soda." She patted her belly. "But I don't mind. It's for a very good cause."

Lucy motioned for them to follow her to the bar that was set up outside.

"*Another* glass?" Jude asked as they made their way to the crowd.

"Lucy and I celebrated with Chelsea and Tori right after we signed the papers this afternoon," Juliette said.

Jude shook his head. "Wow. That was fast. I mean, congratulations, but you just started talking about it earlier this week and it's already finalized?"

"Yes. It was a simple sales contract. The business had no debt. Lucy had quite a bit of money saved. She didn't need to get a loan. So, it was just a matter of getting her attorney to draw up the papers. He did that today. I still need to talk to my landlord to see if I can get out of my lease. Lucy doesn't need the space downtown since she can move it here to the barn. So, for all intents and purposes, the sale is a done deal."

Jude was happy for Juliette and his sister. He really was. That's why he couldn't understand the little pang of… He didn't know what, but a weird feeling nudged at his insides. His little sister—his baby sister—had worked hard and saved enough money to pay cash for her second business. His brother had offered to pay him a salary and the woman he loved was now sitting on a presumably nice-size nest egg after selling a business that she had worked hard to create and grow.

Jude refused to feel sorry for himself, but the truth was, in comparison, he felt every bit the loser that his old man had predicted he would be. He steeled himself. There was no way he was going to fall into a trap of self-pity and self-loathing. He had his options. Now he just needed to get in gear, choose a new path and solidify his new plan.

Nothing like some friendly competition to make him get off his ass.

When they stepped outside, Lucy was behind the bar that was positioned between two tiki torches. They lent a warm glow to the cool, dusky evening. Lucy had commandeered a bottle of sparkling wine and was pouring it into two plastic glasses. She poured herself some club soda and precariously picked up the three beverages and made her way toward them.

Once they all had their drinks, she said, "Here's to bright futures for all three of us. And to the two of you getting back together. I always knew you were meant for each other."

Okay, Lucy might have just been being Lucy, but now she was bordering on making them uncomfortable. Tonight was supposed to be fun, no pressure.

"Juliette and I are still trying to figure things out." Jude eyed his date to see if he could get a read on her. Just as he suspected, she was looking a little uncomfortable. "But everything's going to be okay. I have faith that it will."

He wanted to add that he had enough faith and love for both of them, but at the last minute decided against it. That was implied. It went without saying.

"So have you talked about how you'll handle the long-distance thing?" Lucy asked.

Juliette's mouth tightened. She seemed to give Lucy a look. His protectiveness came out.

"Come on, Lucy, don't put so much pressure on us. Like I said, we're figuring it out. I may have a plan so that we don't need to have to do the long distance—at least not for too long—but we're not there yet."

Lucy looked confused. "I wasn't talking about you. I was talking about Juliette moving to London. Didn't you tell him about the job with Tori?"

Jude blinked, feeling foolish at being caught unaware of what was going on in the life of the woman he loved. "You're moving to London? Since when?"

"Uh-oh," said Lucy. "I didn't realize you two hadn't talked about this yet."

Something in her demeanor told him his sister knew exactly what she was doing. She was forcing them to talk about this because she probably sensed that Juliette had been reluctant.

"No, Lucy, I hadn't told him that, either. I hadn't had a chance and I didn't think tonight at the reunion would be a good time."

Lucy rolled her eyes. "Well, y'all are a couple of nincompoops. Clearly you need to talk this out. I had a feeling if I left it to the two of you, Juliette might be in London before you realized what happened." She gave her brother's arm a gentle push.

"I need to go check on some things," said Lucy. "I'll leave you two to talk amongst yourselves."

They stood in stinging silence for a moment. "So, London, huh?"

"Tori is starting a new wedding division of her design house. She wants me to head it up. That means I'll need to be in London where her offices are located."

Jude was speechless. His vision was a little white and fuzzy around the edges. Was he really watching history really repeat itself? Because from his vantage point, it sure seemed that way. For the second time, just when they were trying to figure things out, she was leaving the country.

"Is this really what you want?" he asked.

Chapter Twelve

What did she want?

Juliette wanted Jude. But she knew they couldn't continue to live the snow globe existence they'd pretended was real life since he'd come back to Celebration.

Some people searched for love their entire lives and never found it. Others found it and the timing never seemed to be right. Since Jude had been home, it had become obvious to Juliette that she and Jude fit into the latter category.

Being star-crossed lovers was not nearly as romantic in real life as it was in romance novels.

It hurt.

It was breaking her heart almost more than when she thought she'd lost Jude to Glori. In both instances, she couldn't have the man she loved. But when the competition was another woman, at least it seemed like she might have a shot if she tried to win him back. Back then she'd been too young, too immature to realize she needed to fight for him.

So she let him go.

But now? How could she compete with Jude's dreams? She knew that if he didn't compete this next year—if he gave it up for her—he would always wonder what if… He'd always regret it and he might even grow to resent her for coming between him and the shot to regain his title.

She wasn't going to keep him from his dreams.

He was a grown man. He knew the risks he was taking by riding against doctors' orders. But that didn't mean she had to stand by and watch him do it. The best place for her right now was in London, where, she hoped, out of sight would mean out of mind.

Fat chance.

She could've throttled Lucy for opening this can of worms tonight. She hadn't been ready to tell him and she had hoped that they could have one more good night together before she did, because she knew he wouldn't be happy about it.

Of course, he would be happy for her. He just wouldn't be happy about the distance.

The band had switched gears to a slow song.

"Is that what I want?" She repeated Jude's question to him because she really didn't know the answer. "All I know right now is that I want to dance with you. Will you dance with me, Jude?"

He had heartbreak in his eyes, or maybe it was her

own feelings mirrored back to her. He took her hand and led her to the dance floor where a handful of couples had the same idea and were swaying together to the band's cover of Blake Shelton's "Mine Would Be You."

Jude pulled her close and they held each other like they would never let each other go. If only that could be true. She clung to him with the same resolve she felt in him.

Love shouldn't be this hard.

It should be so simple. A woman loves a man, a man loves a woman—and they make it work. Somehow, they make it work. Why did making it work feel like such a monumental task?

Juliette lost herself in his arms and for a few glorious moments she was able to shut out the world and her fear that their time was almost up. Then the song ended. Jude stepped back and looked down at her.

"Let's go outside," he said. "We need to talk about this."

Jude took Juliette by the hand and led her out the open side doors, past the cars parked in the parking area, to Lucy's house that she shared with Zane. The place was dark. Zane must've been out for the evening while Lucy was working.

Jude walked up the porch steps and gestured to the cushion-covered front porch swing. Juliette sat down and crossed her arms in front of her because she was chilly. The wrap she had brought wasn't meant for an evening on a dark front porch. As if reading her mind, Jude took off his jacket, draped it around her shoulders. He slid in beside her.

"When were you going to tell me?" he asked.

The moon was bright and she could see his hurt expression illuminated in the glow. She could hear the faint sound of the music emanating from the barn. The band was playing a faster song, but she couldn't quite put her finger on what it was called. It didn't matter.

"Soon." Juliette knew her voice sounded defensive. "But I have to be honest, I wasn't going to tell you tonight and I'm not real happy with your sister for spilling the beans. But I'll talk to her about that later. Jude, Tori just offered me the job this afternoon. It's still new to me."

"Does that mean you haven't yet made up your mind whether you're going to take it or not?"

She shrugged. "It's a great opportunity. Do you know how many women would stand in line for this opportunity?"

"Probably the same women who would've stood in line for your scholarship to St Andrews." Jude raked his hand through his hair and fisted it into the strands above his temples.

It was true. Many of the same people who would've coveted her scholarship would kill for the chance to work for Tori Ashford Alden Designs. Heck, a month ago—three weeks ago—before Jude came back into her life and changed everything—she would've given anything for the chance to leave the unfulfilling wedding planning business for the greener pastures of an international design house.

But that was before Jude had come back.

Now she was torn.

"You're right. Probably those exact same women."

They sat silently for a moment. The squeak of the swing was like a metronome over the music in the barn. Or like a countdown registering the time they were wasting sitting here like this.

"Then why is it that we can't seem to get it together when we are together?" she said. "It's clear to me that you don't want to stay in Celebration—"

"And you said the reason you couldn't come with me was because you *wanted to stay* in Celebration. How do you think it makes me feel to know that you're running back to Europe at the very first chance? Jules, it feels like history is repeating itself all over again. How am I supposed to take that? You won't go with me, but you'll leave me again like you did the first time?"

She closed her eyes and tried to focus on the swing's gentle back-and-forth motion, trying to calm herself with each glide, but it wasn't working.

"Moving to London is different than going on the road with you. You have to be able to see the difference, Jude. In London I will have a purpose. I'll be doing something. I won't simply be following my boyfriend from competition to competition, holding my breath and closing my eyes every time he gets on a bull, praying that this time won't be the time that finally breaks him.

"I told you I was road weary. *I am* road weary. But there's a difference between living out of a suitcase, going from town to town—like I've been doing for five years now with my wedding planning business—and moving somewhere. I'm tired of that, Jude. I'm twenty-eight years old. I need roots. I want a family. I need to come home every night to…"

She shook her head and swiped at a tear that was threatening to betray her. "And why is this all my fault? You could stay. But I know you don't want to."

He blew out a breath.

"The perverse part about this is I came here tonight thinking I had a plan. One that would allow me to stay here with you. But now…"

"What was the plan?"

He shrugged. "It doesn't matter now. The rodeo school will keep," he said. "Since you won't be here, I might as well do the circuit one more year. With the money I can make, I'll be that much better off."

He sounded hurt, as if she'd betrayed him in the worst possible way. But he also sounded like he'd made up his mind.

"Is that what you want, Jude?" she asked. "Or is this your way of punishing me? Telling me you came here with a plan to stay, but now you won't tell me because lo and behold, now you've decided that you're going back on the road. Imagine that."

He braced his forearms on his knees and stared at her for a solid fifteen seconds without saying a word.

"When you left me the first time, you broke my heart," he said. "You were my life. You were the only woman I ever loved. Hell, you were the only person I felt like I could ever really trust. You broke my heart, Juliette. But even after you did, I still wasn't able to move on."

"You know I care about you with all my heart," Juliette said. "But it's not fair for you to pin all the damage and heartbreak on me. You had plenty of opportunities to move on and plenty of time to get over me. You found Glori, didn't you?"

Her tears were flowing now and she wasn't even trying to stop them.

"I did have plenty of opportunities. I've dated plenty of women, but none of them were you. I guess the joke was on me because it seems like you've already moved on. I guess we both have our answers. Now maybe we can both move on."

"I have good news," Bob said around the large bite of burger he was chewing as he talked. "Clive Curtis at Copenhagen has agreed to keep the charitable donation in the On-Off clothing contract intact."

Jude was in Las Vegas having lunch with his agent. The news was good. So why wasn't Jude happy to have an opportunity to throw himself into something this year while he worked to reclaim his title and go out on top?

Why? Because his head hurt and when he'd gotten up this morning his body had ached in that way that was becoming a maddening fact of life. Some mornings when he woke up he felt like if a bull tossed him, his bones might shatter into a million irreparable pieces. He knew this was no way to live. And if he continued to ride it would probably get worse.

"But wait, it gets better," Bob continued. "Copenhagen is willing to use that charitable bit in the promo. They think it might help boost sales. They realized it will make them look good. I'll make sure we get it in the contract that they have to do some PR to get the word out that the charity thing is your idea. We'll make it known that it's your hard-earned money that's going to the needy kids, not Copenhagen's buck."

A surge of irritation coursed through Jude. "Bob. I don't want any recognition for making a donation. I don't want to use children to boost my image."

"Suit yourself, but if you don't grab the credit you know Copenhagen will."

"I don't know why it has to be about grabbing credit. It shouldn't be if you're doing it for the right reasons."

Bob laughed and licked his fingers. "Okay. That right there—that naïveté is part of your charm. No wonder the ladies love you."

There was only one lady in the world whose love mattered and she had chosen to move to London. It should have been enough to stick a fork in their relationship, but Jude still wasn't done. He still couldn't give up on her, and if that meant letting her go to London to work for Tori, then so be it. It would give him a chance to get his own ducks in order, and then he might even go over there and get her. Or at least let her know that he'd be there when she was ready.

"So anyway, Copenhagen said they might be willing to discuss possible sponsorship of that riding school of yours if you win the world championship next year. But there are some pretty strict stipulations and contingencies. You know how Copenhagen is. They are not going to give away anything unless it benefits Copenhagen. But the specifics will be another conversation for another day and we will talk about that when the time comes. But it's something. Another prize for you to keep your eye on this year. See, this is when being a champ really pays off. We can ask for the good stuff. But first things first. I have the contract here."

Bob picked up a manila folder that was lying next to him on the booth bench and slid it across the table toward Jude. "Go ahead and sign it while you're here. Once things get rocking and rolling at the Expo, we might not get to take care of business." Bob took a ballpoint pen out of his shirt pocket and tossed it onto the table.

Jude opened the folder and gazed at the familiar Copenhagen logo emblazoned on the top of the contract. He started to read through all the legalese mumbo jumbo. When he got to the bottom of the first page, he realized he hadn't retained a single word of what he had just read. His attention kept being diverted by the voice in his head that said, *What are you doing, man? Your body hurts. Your heart's not in this nearly as much as it was when you won the championship the first time around. You're not hungry enough to pull it off again.*

The thing that was the most distracting was when he realized this wasn't just negative self talk—his heart really wasn't in it. He didn't even want to be here—signing his life away, maybe even literally—to a company that really didn't care if he lived or died or ended up in some sort of lame limbo in between. He was only important to them as long as he was making them money. He wasn't feeling sorry for himself. He knew that was the honest-to-God truth. He had been a commodity when he was winning and a liability when he'd stopped. Maybe they were crazy to take a chance on him again, at his age and the physical condition he was in.

Suddenly being back in Celebration working for Ethan at the Triple C seemed like the only viable plan.

Even if Juliette was in London he still wanted to be in Celebration. Of course, it would've been better if she were there, but he loved her enough to know he had to let her come to that conclusion on her own, to choose Celebration in a similar way that he had. He'd come all the way to Vegas to realize there was no place like home.

He closed the folder and slid it back across the table toward Bob.

"You didn't sign it." Bob tried to push it back, but Jude put his hand on the folder.

"I'm not signing it. I'm not going to ride again. I will fulfill my last contractual obligation to Copenhagen this weekend at the expo—Curtis said I could sign autographs if I didn't feel like riding. I don't feel like riding. I'm done. Consider me retired."

It was the most freeing feeling in the world to say those three words and mean them. No hesitation. He knew what he wanted.

He may have fallen off the circuit this year and wasn't able to defend his title, but at least he'd gone down as the world champion. No matter what, the title was his. It was something no one could take away from him. Not Copenhagen. And certainly not his dad.

His father had told him he'd never accomplish anything remotely like that, but he'd done it, sometimes despite himself.

He may not be the current champion, but he would always be a champion.

It was time to take what he had learned and put it to good use. The first thing to do was to stop living in the past.

There was a great turnout for the autographing. It was vindicating to know that fans would still line up around the building for him to sign their On-Off Shirts, posters and programs.

Or at least it was fun for the first hour or so. Then it got a little tedious. It was the same drill: "Hey, who would you like me to sign this to?" Occasionally, he would have to ask the person to spell the name. Because if a person waited in line that long to see him, the least he could do was make sure he spelled their name right.

There was still a pretty good line with only about five minutes left in his appearance obligation, so his handlers were moving people through at a pretty good clip. Toward the end, he barely had a chance to look up at a person before the next one was hustled through and he was asking the same question all over again.

This time, the person in front of him laid down a simple piece of paper with a message on it: "Jude, will you marry me?"

He got those occasionally, but this was the first one today. He smiled, but he didn't look up.

"Hey, who would you like me to sign this to?"

"Juliette, please. That's with two *T*s and an *E* on the end."

In the split second between her speaking and him looking up to see if his ears were playing tricks on him, the sound of her voice made every cell in his body stand at attention.

He looked up to find Juliette—his Juliette—standing in front of him. The message on the note that she had handed him registered. He glanced back down to make sure he had read it correctly. He had. He looked back up at her to gauge her reaction.

She was smiling at him. "Well? What's it going to be, cowboy? Are you going to disappoint me after I've come all this way? I've always wanted a Vegas wedding."

"Are you serious?" he asked. "Are you proposing to me?"

She shrugged. "And what would you say if I was?"

"I'd say, I'm sorry folks," he called to the remaining people in line. "I appreciate you waiting for me, but I'm going to have to leave now. This beautiful lady right here just asked me to marry her and I said yes. I let her get away once, and I try to never make the same mistake twice. So if you'll excuse me, I am going to get married."

The crowd erupted into cheers and whistles as Jude hopped over the table and pulled Juliette into his arms and kissed his bride-to-be.

Two hours later, they were standing at the altar in the Little Elvis Wedding Chapel off Las Vegas Boulevard. "Elvis," who was officiating their wedding, was just finishing up a tender, if not slightly off-key, version of "Can't Help Falling in Love."

It couldn't have been more perfect if the real Elvis himself had sang it for them—on pitch.

Juliette was wearing a borrowed veil and the dress that she'd worn on the plane when she'd arrived. The veil was her "something borrowed." The bouquet with blue silk flowers, which was part of the wedding package, was her "something blue." The "something new" was her gold wedding band that they'd picked up at a jewelry store on the way to the chapel. But her "something old" had to be her favorite part of this bridal tradition. The "something old" was their love. It had lasted decades and stood the test of time to finally see them uncross their stars and vow to spend the rest of their lives together.

After Elvis pronounced them husband and wife, they made their way down the aisle and through the chapel exit to a rousing rendition of "Burning Love."

With Juliette's suitcase in tow they went back to Jude's hotel. She'd come straight to him from the airport and was still carting around her luggage.

Drunk on the rush of being newly married, they'd gone straight to the room and consummated their brand-new marriage. Afterward, as they lay there blissfully exhausted, tangled up in each other, Jude said, "So how are we going to do this long-distance thing? We can make it work. The only thing that matters is that you're happy."

She nuzzled his neck and settled deeper into the

crook of his shoulder. "That's so sweet of you. I feel like the luckiest woman in the world. There's no doubt that we'll make this work. I guess the first thing we need to figure out is the schedule of where you'll be each week."

"That's easy. I'll be in Celebration, when I'm not in London. I can go back and forth as much as possible. Maybe we can switch off every other weekend."

"Wait, what?" Juliette said. "I'm not going to London. I was talking about your competition schedule."

"You're not going to London?" He pulled away and rose up on one elbow so he could look at her.

Juliette smiled up at him sheepishly. "I'm not. When it came time to board my flight, I couldn't make myself get on the plane. I called Tori and told her I couldn't come." Jude's mouth fell open.

"So you turned down the job?"

"No. I would've, but I didn't have to. Tori said if I was having anxiety about moving, I was welcome to telecommute and come to London for the occasional office visit. She admitted she'd been surprised that I was willing to move and leave you behind."

Jude made a stabbing motion at his heart.

"How was it that everyone but us seemed to recognize that we really are meant to be? They all saw it long before you and I finally let ourselves believe it."

"Yeah, we finally got a clue like, what, five hours ago?" he joked.

"I told Tori that initially I thought moving would be good for me since you'll be on the road—"

"I'm not going on the road," Jude said.

Juliette wasn't sure if she was understanding him correctly.

"What about the circuit and the Copenhagen sponsorship?"

Jude crooked the elbow of his free arm and shrugged. "Bob gave me the contract today, but maybe it was similar to the way you couldn't get on that plane—I couldn't sign. What kind of an idiot would I be to risk injuring myself—possibly hurting myself to the extent that I couldn't make love to you? I want a life with you. I want to have babies with you. I want to grow old with you."

She melted into his arms. He told her about Ethan's generous offer and how he would be working as a foreman at the Triple C while he got the rodeo school up and running. Jude's next step would be to establish his own legacy—their legacy—right in the middle of his family's land.

"The only thing that could make that homecoming any better would be to come home with my wife."

He kissed her slowly and tenderly. When they finally came up for air, Juliette said, "We're going to make that happen. Because, cowboy, I'm never letting you get away again."

* * * * *

*Catch up with everyone in Celebration with the other
books in the CELEBRATION, TX miniseries!*

*A BRIDE, A BARN, AND A BABY
THE COWBOY'S RUNAWAY BRIDE*

*Available now wherever Harlequin
Special Edition books and ebooks are sold!*

*And if you loved this story, be sure to catch
FORTUNE'S SURPRISE ENGAGEMENT,
Nancy Robards Thompson's contribution to*
THE FORTUNES OF TEXAS:
THE SECRET FORTUNES*!*

*Julia Winston is looking to conquer life,
not become heartbreaker Jamie Caine's
latest conquest. But when two young brothers
wind up in Julia's care for the holidays,
she'll take any help she can get—even Jamie's.*

*Read on for a preview of
New York Times bestselling author
RaeAnne Thayne's SUGAR PINE TRAIL,
the latest installment in her beloved
HAVEN POINT series.*

CHAPTER ONE

THIS WAS GOING to be a disaster.

Julia Winston stood in her front room looking out the lace curtains framing her bay window at the gleaming black SUV parked in her driveway like a sleek, predatory beast.

Her stomach jumped with nerves, and she rubbed suddenly clammy hands down her skirt. Under what crazy moon had she ever thought this might be a good idea? She must have been temporarily out of her head.

Those nerves jumped into overtime when a man stepped out of the vehicle and stood for a moment, looking up at her house.

Jamie Caine.

Tall, lean, hungry.

Gorgeous.

Now the nerves felt more like nausea. What had she done? The moment Eliza Caine called and asked her if her brother-in-law could rent the upstairs apartment of Winston House, she should have told her friend in no uncertain terms that the idea was preposterous. Utterly impossible.

As usual, Julia had been weak and indecisive, and when Eliza told her it was only for six weeks—until January, when the condominium Jamie Caine was buying in a new development along the lake would be finished—she had wavered.

He needed a place to live, and she *did* need the money. Anyway, it was only for six weeks. Surely she could tolerate having the man living upstairs in her apartment for six weeks—especially since he would be out of town for much of those six weeks as part of his duties as lead pilot for the Caine Tech company jet fleet.

The reality of it all was just beginning to sink in, though. Jamie Caine, upstairs from her, in all his sexy, masculine glory.

She fanned herself with her hand, wondering if she was having a premature-onset hot flash or if her new furnace could be on the fritz. The temperature in here seemed suddenly off the charts.

How would she tolerate having him here, spending her evenings knowing he was only a few steps away and that she would have to do her best to hide the absolutely ridiculous, truly humiliating crush she had on the man?

This was such a mistake.

Heart pounding, she watched through the frothy curtains as he pulled a long black duffel bag from the back of his SUV and slung it over his shoulder, lifted a laptop case over the other shoulder, then closed the cargo door and headed for the front steps.

A moment later, her old-fashioned musical doorbell echoed through the house. If she hadn't been so nervous, she might have laughed at the instant reaction of the three cats, previously lounging in various states of boredom around the room. The moment the doorbell rang, Empress and Tabitha both jumped off the sofa as if an electric current had just zipped through it, while Audrey Hepburn arched her back and bushed out her tail.

"That's right, girls. We've got company. It's a man, believe it or not, and he's moving in upstairs. Get ready."

The cats sniffed at her with their usual disdainful look. Empress ran in front of her, almost tripping her on the way to answer the door—on purpose, she was quite sure.

With her mother's cats darting out ahead of her, Julia walked out into what used to be the foyer of the house before she had created the upstairs apartment and now served as an entryway to both residences. She opened the front door, doing her best to ignore the rapid tripping of her heartbeat.

"Hi. You're Julia, right?"

As his sister-in-law was one of her dearest friends, she and Jamie had met numerous times at various events at Snow Angel Cove and elsewhere, but she didn't bother reminding him of that. Julia knew she was eminently forgettable. Most of the time, that was just the way she liked it.

"Yes. Hello, Mr. Caine."

He aimed his high-wattage killer smile at her. "Please. Jamie. Nobody calls me Mr. Caine."

Julia was grimly aware of her pulse pounding in her ears and a strange hitch in her lungs. Up close, Jamie Caine was, in a word, breathtaking. He was Mr. Darcy, Atticus Finch, Rhett Butler and Tom Cruise in *Top Gun* all rolled into one glorious package.

Dark hair, blue eyes and that utterly charming Caine smile he shared with Aidan, Eliza's husband, and the other Caine brothers she had met at various events.

"You were expecting me, right?" he said after an awkward pause. She jolted, suddenly aware she was staring and had left him standing entirely too long on her front step. She was an idiot. "Yes. Of course. Come in. I'm sorry."

Pull yourself together. He's just a guy who happens to be gorgeous.

So far she was seriously failing at Landlady 101. She sucked in a breath and summoned her most brisk keep-your-voice-down-please librarian persona.

"As you can see, we will share the entry. Because the home is on the registry of historical buildings, I couldn't put in an outside entrance to your apartment, as I might have preferred. The house was built in 1880, one of the earliest brick homes on Lake Haven. It was constructed by an ancestor of mine, Sir Robert Winston, who came from a wealthy British family and made his own fortune supplying timber to the railroads. He also invested in one of the first hot-springs resorts in the area. The home is Victorian, specifically in the spindled Queen Anne style. It consists of seven bedrooms and four bathrooms. When those bathrooms were added in the 1920s, they provided some of the first indoor plumbing in the region."

"Interesting," he said, though his expression indicated he found it anything but.

She was rambling, she realized, as she tended to do when she was nervous.

She cleared her throat and pointed to the doorway, where the three cats were lined up like sentinels, watching him with unblinking stares. "Anyway, through those doors is my apartment and yours is upstairs. I have keys to both doors for you along with a packet of information here."

She glanced toward the ornate marble-top table in the entryway—that her mother claimed once graced the mansion of Leland Stanford on Nob Hill in San Francisco—where she thought she had left the information. Unfortunately, it was bare. "Oh. Where did I put that? I must have left it inside in my living room. Just a moment."

The cats weren't inclined to get out of her way, so she stepped over them, wondering if she came across as eccentric to him as she felt, a spinster librarian living with cats in a crumbling house crammed with antiques, a space much too big for one person.

After a mad scan of the room, she finally found the two keys along with the carefully prepared file folder of instructions atop the mantel, nestled amid her collection of porcelain angels. She had no recollection of moving them there, probably due to her own nervousness at having Jamie Caine moving upstairs.

She swooped them up and hurried back to the entry, where she found two of the cats curled around his leg, while Audrey was in his arms, currently being petted by his long, square-tipped fingers.

She stared. The cats had no time for or interest in her. She only kept them around because her mother had adored them, and Julia couldn't bring herself to give away Mariah's adored pets. Apparently no female—human or feline—was immune to Jamie Caine. She should have expected it.

"Nice cats."

Julia frowned. "Not usually. They're standoffish and bad tempered to most people."

"I guess I must have the magic touch."

So the Haven Point rumor mill said about him, anyway. "I guess you do," she said. "I found your keys and information about the apartment. If you would like, I can show you around upstairs."

"Lead on."

He offered a friendly smile, and she told herself that shiver rippling down her spine was only because the entryway was cooler than her rooms.

"This is a lovely house," he said as he followed her up the staircase. "Have you lived here long?"

"Thirty-two years in February. All my life, in other words."

Except the first few days, anyway, when she had still been in the Oregon hospital where her parents adopted her, and the three years she had spent at Boise State.

"It's always been in my family," she continued. "My father was born here and his father before him."

She was a Winston only by adoption but claimed her parents' family trees as her own and respected and admired their ancestors and the elegant home they had built here.

At the second-floor landing, she unlocked the apartment that had been hers until she moved down to take care of her mother after Mariah's first stroke, two years ago. A few years after taking the job at the Haven Point library, she had redecorated the upstairs floor of the house. It had been her way of carving out her own space.

Yes, she had been an adult living with her parents. Even as she might have longed for some degree of independence, she couldn't justify moving out when her mother had so desperately needed her help with Julia's ailing father.

Anyway, she had always figured it wasn't the same as most young adults who lived in their parents' apartments. She'd had an entire self-contained floor to herself. If she wished, she could shop on her own, cook on her own, entertain her friends, all without bothering her parents.

Really, it had been the best of all situations—close enough to help, yet removed enough to live her own life. Then her father died and her mother became frail herself, and Julia had felt obligated to move downstairs to be closer, in case her mother needed her.

Now, as she looked at her once-cherished apartment, she tried to imagine how Jamie Caine would see these rooms, with the graceful reproduction furniture and the pastel wall colors and the soft carpet and curtains.

Oddly, the feminine decorations only served to emphasize how very *male* Jamie Caine was, in contrast.

She did her best to ignore that unwanted observation.

"This is basically the same floor plan as my rooms below, with three bedrooms, as well as the living room and kitchen," she explained. "You've got an en suite bathroom off the largest bedroom and another one for the other two bedrooms."

"Wow. That's a lot of room for one guy."

"It's a big house," she said with a shrug. She had even more room downstairs, factoring in the extra bedroom in one addition and the large south-facing sunroom.

Winston House was entirely too rambling for one single woman and three bad-tempered cats. It had been too big for an older couple and their adopted daughter. It had been too large when it was just her and her mother, after her father died.

The place had basically echoed with emptiness for the better part of a year after her mother's deteriorating condition had necessitated her move to the nursing home in Shelter Springs. Her mother had hoped to return to the house she had loved, but that never happened, and Mariah Winston died four months ago.

Julia missed her every single day.

"Do you think it will work for you?" she asked.

"It's more than I need, but should be fine. Eliza told you this is only temporary, right?"

Julia nodded. She was counting on it. Then she could find a nice, quiet, older lady to rent who wouldn't leave her so nervous.

"She said your apartment lease ran out before your new condo was finished."

"Yes. The development was supposed to be done two months ago, but the builder has suffered delay after delay. I've already extended my lease twice. I didn't want to push my luck with my previous landlady by asking for a third extension."

All Jamie had to do was smile at the woman and she likely would have extended his lease again without quibbling. And probably would have given him anything else he wanted, too.

Julia didn't ask why he chose not to move into Snow Angel Cove with his brother Aidan and Aidan's wife, Eliza, and their children. It was none of her business, anyway. The only thing she cared about was the healthy amount he was paying her in rent, which would just about cover the new furnace she had installed a month earlier.

"It was a lucky break for me when Eliza told me you were considering taking on a renter for your upstairs space."

He aimed that killer smile at her again, and her core muscles trembled from more than just her workout that morning.

If she wasn't very, very careful, she would end up making a fool of herself over the man.

It took effort, but she fought the urge to return his smile. This was business, she told herself. That was all. She had something he needed, a place to stay, and he was willing to pay for it. She, in turn, needed funds if she wanted to maintain this house that had been in her family for generations.

"It works out for both of us. You've already signed the rental agreement outlining the terms of your tenancy and the rules."

She held out the information packet. "Here you'll find all the information you might need, information like internet access, how to work the electronics and the satellite television channels, garbage pickup day and mail delivery. Do you have any other questions?"

Business, she reminded herself, making her voice as no-nonsense and brisk as possible.

"I can't think of any now, but I'm sure something will come up."

He smiled again, but she thought perhaps this time his expression was a little more reserved. Maybe he could sense she was un-charmable.

Or so she wanted to tell herself, anyway.

"I would ask that you please wipe your feet when you carry your things in and out, given the snow out there. The stairs are original wood, more than a hundred years old."

Cripes. She sounded like a prissy spinster librarian.

"I will do that, but I don't have much to carry in. Since El told me the place is furnished, I put almost everything in storage." He gestured to the duffel and laptop bag, which he had set inside the doorway. "Besides this, I've only got a few more boxes in the car."

"In that case, here are your keys. The large one goes to the outside door. The smaller one is for your apartment. I keep the outside door locked at all times. You can't be too careful."

"True enough."

She glanced at her watch. "I'm afraid I've already gone twenty minutes past my lunch hour and must return to the library. My cell number is written on the front of the packet, in case of emergency."

"Looks like you've covered everything."

"I think so." Yes, she was a bit obsessively organized, and she didn't like surprises. Was anything wrong with that?

"I hope you will be comfortable here," she said, then tried to soften her stiff tone with a smile that felt every bit as awkward. "Good afternoon."

"Uh, same to you."

Her heart was still pounding as she nodded to him and hurried for the stairs, desperate for escape from all that…masculinity.

She rushed back downstairs and into her apartment for her purse, wishing she had time to splash cold water on her face.

However would she get through the next six weeks with him in her house?

He was *NOT* looking forward to the next six weeks.

Jamie stood in the corner of the main living space to the apartment he had agreed to rent, sight unseen.

Big mistake.

It was roomy and filled with light, that much was true. But the decor was too…fussy…for a man like him, all carved wood and tufted upholstery and pastel wall colorings.

It wasn't exactly his scene, more like the kind of place a repressed, uppity librarian might live.

As soon as he thought the words, Jamie frowned at himself. That wasn't fair. She might not have been overflowing with warmth and welcome, but Julia Winston had been very polite to him—especially since he knew she hadn't necessarily wanted to rent to him.

This was what happened when he gave his sister-in-law free rein to find him an apartment in the tight local rental market. She had been helping him out, since he had been crazy busy the last few weeks flying Caine Tech execs from coast to coast—and all places in between—as they worked on a couple of big mergers.

Eliza had wanted him to stay at her and Aidan's rambling house by the lake. The place was huge, and they had plenty of room, but while he loved his older brother Aidan and his wife and kids, Jamie preferred his own space. He didn't much care what that space looked like, especially when it was temporary.

With time running out on his lease extension, he had been relieved when Eliza called him via Skype the week before to tell him she had found him something more than suitable, for a decent rent.

"You'll love it!" Eliza had beamed. "It's the entire second floor of a gorgeous old Victorian in that great neighborhood on Snow Blossom Lane, with a simply stunning view of the lake."

"Sounds good," he had answered.

"You'll be upstairs from my friend Julia Winston,

and, believe me, you couldn't ask for a better land-lady. She's sweet and kind and perfectly wonderful. You know Julia, right?"

When he had looked blankly at her and didn't im-mediately respond, his niece Maddie had popped her face into the screen from where she had been appar-ently listening in off camera. "You know! She's the li-brary lady. She tells all the stories!"

"Ah. *That* Julia," he'd said, not bothering to mention to his seven-year-old niece that in more than a year of living in town, he had somehow missed out on story time at the Haven Point library.

He also didn't mention to Maddie's mother that he only vaguely remembered Julia Winston. Now that he had seen her again, he understood why. She was the kind of woman who tended to slip into the background—and he had the odd impression that wasn't accidental.

She wore her brown hair past her shoulders, with-out much curl or style to it and held back with a simple black band, and she appeared to use little makeup to play up her rather average features.

She did have lovely eyes, he had to admit. Extraor-dinary, even. They were a stunning blue, almost violet, fringed by naturally long eyelashes.

Her looks didn't matter, nor did the decor of her house. He would only be here a few weeks; then he would be moving into his new condo.

She clearly didn't like him. He frowned, wondering how he might have offended Julia Winston. He barely remembered even meeting the woman, but he must have done something for her to be so cool to him.

A few times during that odd interaction, she had alternated between seeming nervous to be in the same room with him to looking at him with her mouth pursed tightly, as if she had just caught him spreading peanut butter across the pages of *War and Peace*.

She was entitled to her opinion. Contrary to popular belief, he didn't need everyone to like him.

His brothers would probably say it was good for him to live upstairs from a woman so clearly immune to his charm.

One thing was clear: he now had one more reason to be eager for his condo to be finished.

Don't miss
SUGAR PINE TRAIL
by RaeAnne Thayne
Available October 2017 from HQN Books!

Copyright © 2017 by RaeAnne Thayne

COMING NEXT MONTH FROM

HARLEQUIN®

SPECIAL EDITION

Available October 17, 2017

#2581 THE RANCHER'S CHRISTMAS SONG
The Cowboys of Cold Creek • by RaeAnne Thayne
Music teacher Ella Baker doesn't have time to corral rancher Beckett McKinley's two wild boys. But when they ask her to teach them a song for their father, she manages to wrangle some riding lessons out of the deal. Still, Ella and Beckett come from two different worlds, and it might take a Christmas miracle to finally bring them together.

#2582 THE MAVERICK'S SNOWBOUND CHRISTMAS
Montana Mavericks: The Great Family Roundup
by Karen Rose Smith
Rancher Eli Dalton believes that visiting vet Hadley Strickland is just the bride he's been searching for! But can he heal her broken heart in time for the perfect holiday proposal?

#2583 A COWBOY FAMILY CHRISTMAS
Rocking Chair Rodeo • by Judy Duarte
When Drew Madison, a handsome rodeo promoter, meets the temporary cook at the Rocking Chair Ranch, the avowed bachelor falls for the lovely Lainie Montoya. But things get complicated when he learns she's the mystery woman who broke up his sister's marriage!

#2584 SANTA'S SEVEN-DAY BABY TUTORIAL
Hurley's Homestyle Kitchen • by Meg Maxwell
When FBI agent Colt Asher, who's been left with his baby nephews for ten days before Christmas, needs a nanny, he hires Anna Miller, a young Amish woman on *rumspringa* trying to decide if she wants to remain in the outside world or return to her Amish community.

#2585 HIS BY CHRISTMAS
The Bachelors of Blackwater Lake • by Teresa Southwick
Calhoun Hart was planning on filling his forced vacation with adventure and extreme sports until he broke his leg. Now he's stuck on a beautiful tropical island working with Justine Walker to get some business done on the sly—and is suddenly falling for the calm, collected woman with dreams of her own.

#2586 THEIR CHRISTMAS ANGEL
The Colorado Fosters • by Tracy Madison
When widowed single father Parker Lennox falls for his daughters' music teacher, he quickly discovers there's also a baby in the mix—and it isn't his! To complicate matters further, Nicole survived the same cancer that took his wife. Can Santa deliver Parker and Nicole the family they both want for Christmas this year?

YOU CAN FIND MORE INFORMATION ON UPCOMING HARLEQUIN® TITLES, FREE EXCERPTS AND MORE AT WWW.HARLEQUIN.COM.

HSECNM1017

Get 2 Free Books,

Plus 2 Free Gifts—
just for trying the
Reader Service!

HARLEQUIN®

SPECIAL EDITION

YES! Please send me 2 FREE Harlequin® Special Edition novels and my 2 FREE gifts (gifts are worth about $10 retail). After receiving them, if I don't wish to receive any more books, I can return the shipping statement marked "cancel." If I don't cancel, I will receive 6 brand-new novels every month and be billed just $4.99 per book in the U.S. or $5.74 per book in Canada. That's a savings of at least 12% off the cover price! It's quite a bargain! Shipping and handling is just 50¢ per book in the U.S. and 75¢ per book in Canada.* I understand that accepting the 2 free books and gifts places me under no obligation to buy anything. I can always return a shipment and cancel at any time. The free books and gifts are mine to keep no matter what I decide.

235/335 HDN GLWR

Name _____ (PLEASE PRINT)

Address _____ Apt. #

City _____ State/Province _____ Zip/Postal Code

Signature (if under 18, a parent or guardian must sign)

Mail to the **Reader Service:**
IN U.S.A.: P.O. Box 1341, Buffalo, NY 14240-8531
IN CANADA: P.O. Box 603, Fort Erie, Ontario L2A 5X3

Want to try two free books from another line?
Call 1-800-873-8635 or visit www.ReaderService.com.

*Terms and prices subject to change without notice. Prices do not include applicable taxes. Sales tax applicable in N.Y. Canadian residents will be charged applicable taxes. Offer not valid in Quebec. This offer is limited to one order per household. Books received may not be as shown. Not valid for current subscribers to Harlequin Special Edition books. All orders subject to approval. Credit or debit balances in a customer's account(s) may be offset by any other outstanding balance owed by or to the customer. Please allow 4 to 6 weeks for delivery. Offer available while quantities last.

Your Privacy—The Reader Service is committed to protecting your privacy. Our Privacy Policy is available online at www.ReaderService.com or upon request from the Reader Service.

We make a portion of our mailing list available to reputable third parties that offer products we believe may interest you. If you prefer that we not exchange your name with third parties, or if you wish to clarify or modify your communication preferences, please visit us at www.ReaderService.com/consumerschoice or write to us at Reader Service Preference Service, P.O. Box 9062, Buffalo, NY 14240-9062. Include your complete name and address.

HSE17R2

SPECIAL EXCERPT FROM

H HARLEQUIN®

SPECIAL EDITION

™

*Ella Baker is trading music lessons for riding
lessons from the wild twin McKinley boys—but it's
their father who would need a Christmas miracle to
let Ella into his heart.*

*Read on for a sneak preview of
the RANCHER'S CHRISTMAS SONG,
the next book in* New York Times *bestselling author*
RaeAnne Thayne's *beloved miniseries*
THE COWBOYS OF COLD CREEK.

Beckett finally spoke. "Uh, what seems to be the trouble?"

His voice had an odd, strangled note to it. Was he
laughing at her? When she couldn't see him, Ella couldn't
be quite sure. "It's stuck in my hair comb. I don't want
to rip the sweater—or yank out my hair, for that matter."

He paused again, then she felt the air stir as he moved
closer. The scent of him was stronger now, masculine and
outdoorsy, and everything inside her sighed a welcome.

He stood close enough that she could feel the heat
radiating from him. She caught her breath, torn between
a completely prurient desire for the moment to last at
least a little longer and a wild hope that the humiliation
of being caught in this position would be over quickly.

"Hold still," he said. Was his voice deeper than usual?
She couldn't quite tell. She did know it sent tiny delicious
shivers down her spine.

"You've really done a job here," he said after a
moment.

"I know. I'm not quite sure how it tangled so badly."

She would have to breathe soon or she was likely to pass out. She forced herself to inhale one breath and then another until she felt a little less light-headed.

"Almost there," he said, his big hands in her hair, then a moment later she felt a tug and the sweater slipped all the way over her head.

"There you go."

"Thank you." She wanted to disappear, to dive under that great big log bed and hide away. Instead, she forced her mouth into a casual smile. "These Christmas sweaters can be dangerous. Who knew?"

She was blushing. She could feel her face heat and wondered if he noticed. This certainly counted among the most embarrassing moments of her life.

"Want to explain again what you're doing in my bedroom, tangled up in your clothes?" he asked.

She frowned at his deliberately risqué interpretation of something that had been innocent. Mostly.

There had been that secret moment when she had closed her eyes and imagined being here with him under that soft quilt, but he had no way of knowing that.

She folded up her sweater, wondering if she would ever be able to look the man in the eye again.

Don't miss
THE RANCHER'S CHRISTMAS SONG
by RaeAnne Thayne,
available November 2017 wherever
Harlequin® Special Edition books and ebooks are sold.

www.Harlequin.com

Copyright © 2017 by RaeAnne Thayne

EXCLUSIVE
Limited Time Offer

$1.00 OFF

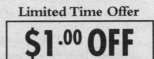

New York Times Bestselling Author

RaeAnne Thayne

SUGAR PINE TRAIL

*An unlikely attraction brings comfort, joy and
unforgettable romance this holiday season!*

*Available September 26, 2017.
Pick up your copy today!*

HQN™

$7.99 U.S./$9.99 CAN.

$1.00 OFF   the purchase price of SUGAR PINE TRAIL by RaeAnne Thayne.

Offer valid from September 26, 2017 to October 31, 2017.
Redeemable at participating retail outlets. Not redeemable at Barnes & Noble.
Limit one coupon per purchase. Valid in the U.S.A. and Canada only.

52615030

5 65373 00076 2   (8100)0 12300

Canadian Retailers: Harlequin Enterprises Limited will pay the face value of this coupon plus 10.25¢ if submitted by customer for this product only. Any other use constitutes fraud. Coupon is nonassignable. Void if taxed, prohibited or restricted by law. Consumer must pay any government taxes. Void if copied. Inmar Promotional Services ("IPS") customers submit coupons and proof of sales to Harlequin Enterprises Limited, P.O. Box 31000, Scarborough, ON M1R 0E7, Canada. Non-IPS retailer—for reimbursement submit coupons and proof of sales directly to Harlequin Enterprises Limited, Retail Marketing Department, 225 Duncan Mill Rd., Don Mills, ON M3B 3K9, Canada.

U.S. Retailers: Harlequin Enterprises Limited will pay the face value of this coupon plus 8¢ if submitted by customer for this product only. Any other use constitutes fraud. Coupon is nonassignable. Void if taxed, prohibited or restricted by law. Consumer must pay any government taxes. Void if copied. For reimbursement submit coupons and proof of sales directly to Harlequin Enterprises, Ltd 482, NCH Marketing Services, P.O. Box 880001, El Paso, TX 88588-0001, U.S.A. Cash value 1/100 cents.

® and ™ are trademarks owned and used by the trademark owner and/or its licensee.

© 2017 Harlequin Enterprises Limited

PHCOUPRATSE1017

Looking for more satisfying love stories
with community and family at their core?

Check out **Harlequin® Special Edition**
and **Harlequin® Western Romance** books!

New books available every month!

CONNECT WITH US AT:

Harlequin.com/Community

 Facebook.com/HarlequinBooks

Twitter.com/HarlequinBooks

Instagram.com/HarlequinBooks

Pinterest.com/HarlequinBooks

ReaderService.com

**ROMANCE WHEN
YOU NEED IT**

HFGENRE2017R

THE WORLD IS BETTER WITH
Romance

Harlequin has everything from contemporary, passionate and heartwarming to suspenseful and inspirational stories.

Whatever your mood, we have a romance just for you!

Connect with us to find your next great read, special offers and more.

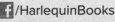 /HarlequinBooks

@HarlequinBooks

www.HarlequinBlog.com

www.Harlequin.com/Newsletters

HARLEQUIN®

A *Romance* FOR EVERY MOOD™

www.Harlequin.com

SERIESHALOAD2015

LOVE
Harlequin
romance?

Join our Harlequin community to share your thoughts and connect with other romance readers!

Be the first to find out about promotions, news, and exclusive content!

Sign up for the Harlequin e-newsletter and download a free book from any series at

www.TryHarlequin.com

CONNECT WITH US AT:

Harlequin.com/Community

 Facebook.com/HarlequinBooks

Twitter.com/HarlequinBooks

Instagram.com/HarlequinBooks

Pinterest.com/HarlequinBooks

ReaderService.com

**ROMANCE WHEN
YOU NEED IT**

HSOCIAL2017